Changing The Heart

PRESENT

MELISSA COBB

A badge gives you authority but does it make you off limits.

NOT CROSS   CRIME SCENE

GIRLS IN BLUE

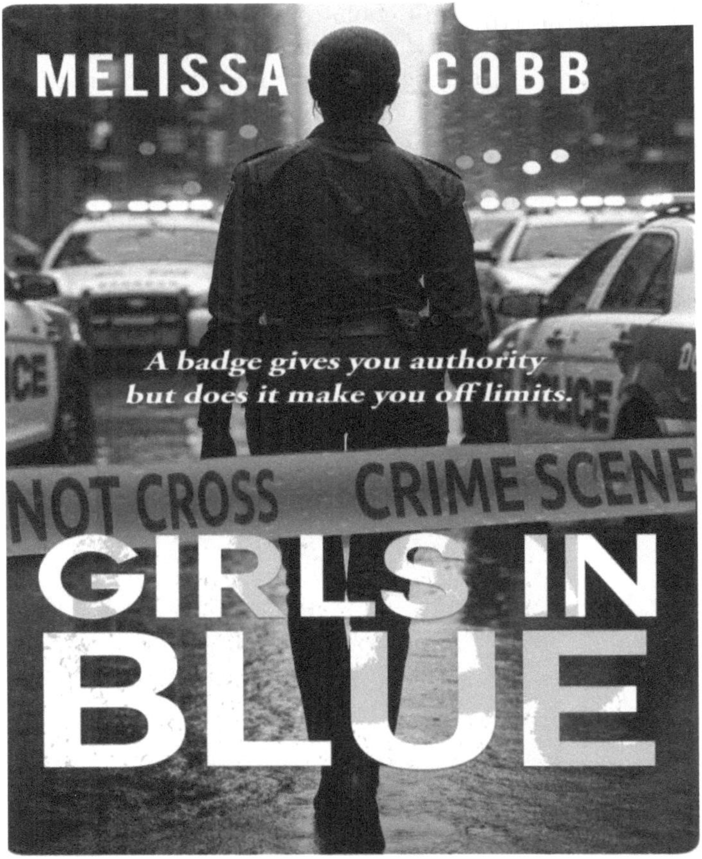

Louisville, Mississippi
GIRLS IN BLUE

ISBN 979-8-9931887-1-3

Printed in the United States

Statement

"When you don't like the direction, you are going; CHANGE DIRECTIONS."

Dedication Page

To my dad: Late Officer Joseph Lee

The actions in this book DOES NOT portray them or ANY other uniform officer. Thank you both for protecting and serving the Mississippi Counties: Scott, Newton, Leake and Hinds.

THE BEGINNING

"You're one damn CHAB."

"Yeah? Well, fuck you too, Ve-Lo and I'm not a coldhearted, hating ass bitch. But, if you think you're the only dick at the party, then I'm at the wrong damn party."

Everybody turned to see what the fuss was all about. I yelled because he just put my heart in my hand. I trusted and loved me some him and gave him anything and everything a man could want. Nothing was out of reach for him. All he had to do was say, "I want," and I went and got it, simple as that. The things I did for him, reached towards the sky and to find out, I was just a side chick. A side chick, when I thought I was the main chick, because I was doing what he needed done.

I couldn't think of a time he didn't get what he wanted from me. I never really thought he would do this to me. I can understand if I wasn't pulling my part, but I was. It might not have been too bad, but he showed up at Jarissa's party with a well-known slut. Of all the women in town, he showed up with her. I see now it doesn't matter what you do for someone, just don't be caught doing the right thing for the wrong one; that's what I did. His ass played me with a hoe move.

But I'm the one who's looking stupid here in front of my folks. There is no sense of fronting her over dick I thought I

1

was the only one getting; got to get my priorities straight. I've got to get me together because I can't afford to fall to pieces ever again. I must admit, I never saw it coming. I really can't get mad at her for coming out as the top player, but I can get even. After seeing them together that day, I vowed to show the world what hell on earth really is. I will show him, and men like him what grown women do. The idiom says, "There is no sense in crying over spilled milk, have your cat to lick it up."

CHAPTER 1

Years Later

"Beast let's go the long way back to the station. When we get there, we will almost be 10-7; in time for us to get off and eat. I know you're hungry, boy, because I'm starving."

My K-9 best friend, Beast, barked with agreement as I glanced over at him. Soon as I turned onto Old Jackson and drove past Scott Central School, I heard Dispatcher Renee's sturdy voice, saying, "Calling all cars, there's a 10-40 in progress at the Northside Convenience Store. The individual is a tall, black male wearing a black outfit, having long black dreads with blue tips. He was seen leaving the crime in a maroon Chevy Lumina, heading north towards Carthage. He is armed and dangerous. I repeat, armed and dangerous."

I radioed, "Beast and I are looking at Highway 35 now, 10-4."

Then, I saw the car as I yelled into the CB, "I see it! 10-4."

I cleared the frequency as I heard Officer Jackson say, "Bell and I copy from Roscoe Lane. We are in pursuit now towards Highway 35 behind Cat."

With my siren and lights on, I drove fast as I could. I wonder who would rob a well-populated store at bright

3

daybreak. Beast began his excitement barking as we followed in pursuit of the car. I noticed there were more individuals in the vehicle. Calling back, I stated, "I have visual on the suspects and there is more than one occupant in the vehicle, 10-4?"

"10-4," Officer Jackson replied, as they drove three car lengths behind me.

Before making it past the North Little River Road in Harperville, the back and passenger side door opened. The individuals began to tumble out. I swerved quickly as I rapidly dispatched back, "They jumping out the car! They jumping out the car!"

"10-9!" Officer Jackson yelled through the CB.

"I repeat, they jumping out the car. You guys get those bastards. I'm following the damn getaway car."

In the rearview mirror, I saw my partners fall back in pursuit of the individuals that bailed. I looked at my speedometer, noticing it's registering well over one hundred miles on this busy road. I became very angry with the driver. Suddenly, the car took a sharp right onto Robinson Road and flipped. I radioed, "I have a 10-50. Repeat, a 10-50. The vehicle has wrecked while approaching a turn on Robinson Road. 10-4."

"10-4," Renee replied.

Making sure I parked directly behind the overturned car, just as the driver took off down the dirt road. "Fuck, he's running," I yelled to myself. Snatching the gear into park, I unleashed Beast and screamed, "Get that ass!" I took off behind him as I screamed into my body radio, between rapid breaths, "I'm in foot pursuit on Robinson Road!"

Beast was in full throttle behind the suspect as I kept my eyes on him. I'm pissed because the suspect is fast, like a deer escaping from a hunter. With me behind the assailant, I ran for another two hundred yards before Beast leaped into the air and caught him by the right arm. When Beast latched onto him, the suspect fell face-first onto the ground, screaming, "Tell ya dog to let me go!"

Running a little faster, I quickly made it to the scene. Placing my hands on my knees, I had to slow my breathing first. Recovering quickly from the fast-paced exercise, I lost it. With Beast still maintaining his bite and hold, I walked over to him and kicked the accused robber a few times near the ribs. He yelled out, "You crazy! You fucking kicking me."

The thing with me is, I know how to hit a perp, so nothing shows up; however, I wasn't giving a damn in this instance. This young punk endangered my life, as well as his and Beast's. For that, there is no remorse. I placed my knee down hard in his back, while applying a lot of pressure on him.

5

I literally pressed his body print in the ground. Snatching the individual's left arm down, I thought about how his young dumb ass has now forced me to have paperwork to do before I could go home. I have things going on and now my thing involves him. Feeling angrier, I handcuffed the left arm first, then screamed, "Beast, down! Beast, let him go so I could place the right hand in the cuffs."

In rage, I jerked upward and jolted the tall, puny youngster onto his feet. I placed him in front of me as he screamed, "You hurting me, you short bitch!"

Once he said that, I hit him behind his knee, and he fell on his knees. I responded, "That's for carelessly endangering our lives. I know you won't, but I hope you rot in jail for resisting arrest, reckless driving, and failure to stop at blue lights. Let's go, Beast."

I snatched the teen upward on his feet and made sure Beast was behind us in case he ran again. The lying little boy yelled out, "I ain't do shit. I should press charges against you for hitting me, because I'm a black man looking suspect to the pigs!"

I'm abusing him and he's threatening me, I questioned in my mind as he rambled on and on, saying, "You lucky I flipped. If I hadn't wrecked, I was taking you down through there and fuck you up. I was going to teach you police a lesson about harassment."

Deciding to show him real abuse, I took my leg and tripped him hard. The suspect fell face-first on the dirt road, mixed with fresh rocks. Beast grabbed his foot. He screamed out, "What's wrong with you? What the hell wrong with you and your dog?"

Having enough of his mouth and attitude, I took out my gun and deliberately fell onto him with all the weight I had. He hollered out loudly, but I didn't care. I should, but since I mean business, I placed the muzzle hard against his head. He realized what it was and spat, "What's wrong with you? You trying to fucking kill me?"

In a quiet but meaningful tone, I stated, "Shut your stealing ass up and stop resisting the fucking arrest. I'm the hoe, and you the client that just got fucked. I will say you tried to kill me, and no damn judge anywhere in the land will convict me, because you are one less product of our environment that is off the streets. Now, shut the hell up before I blow your brains out your head and call it a day. I'm tired, hungry, and have things planned when I get home. Paperwork is nothing, while your ass lay cold in a morgue for your family to identify the rest of your body."

I could feel him shaking as I spoke of killing him. Seeing I made my point, I got up off him and put my gun in the holster. I yelled, "Beast, down," as I yanked him up. "Now, I'm adding threatening an officer with the rest of your charges."

The young chap didn't say another word. We made it back within view of the car and Beast began barking. In sight, my fellow workers had apprehended the other three suspects and were checking on me. I put on my gloves and got out the markers. He had his camera out, so I didn't need mine. I looked up as he stated, "I thought you were 10-7?"

"I was going off duty. In fact, I was taking Highway 35 back so when I got there, all I had to do is clock out and go home. Now, look at this mess."

"You going home alright, right after you finish this paperwork," my co-worker joked.

"You too. I won't be there alone."

Reaching down inside the car he got up saying, "Look what I found."

It was a pound of marijuana, a cookie of crack cocaine and a bunch of smashed-up money; I assume from the robbery. Bell took the pictures as we placed the evidence in the bag. Other state troopers came onto the scene because the incident occurred on the state highway. I got in my patrol car and dispatched in. "I have a J-1, and I'm headed back. 10-4?"

"10-4," Renee stated back to me.

The thief said, "Please don't let your dog hurt me."

"That's not up to me, that's up to Beast. For all I know, he hurt you because you were picking at him, or you want your family to get some type of money because of your fuck-up."

He didn't say another word as he clung near the door. I drove off, knowing Beast was watching the teen and keeping him in check. The entire trip, the youngster kept his head facing the window and didn't say a word. I guess reality was setting in about him being locked up and facing his crimes. I arrived at the station and took Beast out first and tied him in the area for dogs; then I took the suspect in for booking. Renee asked as she swayed her head, "He must have worn you out?"

"No, I'm pissed. I can't go home and sleep like I wanted, because his ass wants things that are not his. Then, he made me run after him."

She laughed as I handed him over for processing and began the paperwork. Moments later, Bell and Jackson brought the others in for processing. Bell asked, "He outran you, didn't he?"

"Why should I run when I have Beast?"

"So, Beast doing your dirty work?"

9

"Funny, but my best friend does his job, now go do yours."

"Ooh, that was cold, Hell Cat."

"No, cold is I'm about finished with my paperwork, and you haven't started on yours."

Thirty minutes later, I clocked out and unhooked Beast and we went home. Soon as I got there, I fed Beast and let him loose on the yard. I'm tired, but with him running around, no one will bother me or steal him. Unlocking the door, I turned off my alarm, locked my door back, took a hot bath and slept very soundlessly for nine hours.

When I woke up, I checked on Beast, he was lying on the steps. I saw the way the sunlight hit my truck and realized just how dirty it was. Shaking my head, I went back in, put on some comfortable clothes, and got my keys off the key rack. I set my alarm and called for Beast because he had moved from the steps. He came like I knew he would, and we rode to Northside for pizza and to wash my truck.

Soon as I arrived, I went in and ordered my pizza, bought a soda, and paid for the gas. I waited for ten minutes and brought the pizza back out with me before I pumped gas. I drove around the building and let Beast urinate on the ground before we began eating the pizza. Once we finished, Beast jumped on the back as I pulled up in a wash stall. Lo and behold, coming by me was a yellow Nissan Altima. It slowed down but kept going, as we checked each other out.

The passenger got out and went in the store. Paying them no more attention, I loaded the machine with the quarters. Beast started barking feverishly. I walked towards the back of my truck, but I didn't see him. When I walked on around the truck to the front, Beast was in the front. I yelled at my blue pit bull, "Beast, stand down!" He stopped barking but stood at attention.

Turning my head back around, I saw three women. The tallest of the trio stood about two feet from me and spoke like she had balls. "You the type of bitch that can't be high classed with your broke ass."

I don't know her, and I think she has me confused. I looked around and asked her girls as I pointed my finger, "Excuse me, you broke bitches see who this broke bitch is talking to?"

They didn't respond. I focused my attention at the tall woman who spoke by saying, "Stay away from my man, Texan. He has a child to feed and a woman that loves him."

I laughed and asked, "You talking about that weak motherfucker that just filled my gas tank up? If you want that type of man; go right on. I don't need his little dick ass, but if he comes with that bread; don't think I won't get it. As for you

11

and your child eating, the hell with y'all. I wouldn't care if y'all go hungry because this bitch got to eat too."

"You no better than a hoe on the corner."

"Say what the hell you want. I'm getting me and from the look of it; I'm getting yours too." I stated directly at her face, with a smile. "Seems like you like talking. I don't have all day for that. I have things to do and places to go. I'm either going to kick your ass and those thrown-away-looking bitches can help you, or I will kick your ass and leave you where you lay. Choose?"

When she didn't jump, I did. I went for her stomach with an open fist because the closer there is contact; you close your fist, and the pressure will be more damageable. As soon as she crouched over holding her stomach, I snatched her under her throat with my right hand and applied pressure. My left hand swung tediously at her brain for a change of thinking. Her girls came towards me, but Beast made his existence known by barking and growling at the suspects. He adopted a guarding stance as he awaited my orders.

Seeing she didn't have quite enough; I squeezed her throat a little more before releasing. She couldn't do anything because she couldn't breathe. It's like holding your breath. You won't die from holding your breath, but you can have some brain damage if done long enough. I noticed she was on the brink of passing out, so I let her go. The lady began gasping for breath as she fell on the concrete ground and sat there. Her girls saw her and couldn't help her because Beast was still on guard. Giving her a final look, I yelled, "Beast, in."

Beast jumped back into the truck and repositioned himself in his attention stance. I walked backwards to my brand-new, four-door, white Dodge truck. I proclaimed loudly as I drove off, "Stupid bitch. You don't fight over dick. You suck it or fuck it!"

Normally, I don't have any altercations because my men usually keep their hoes under control. The main woman is their problem, not mine, but shit happens every so often. I know it's true when hoes fall in love, they fall out of line. It's no longer his problem now, it's mine and I don't take kindly to handling other people's business. I shook my head as the thought crossed my mind, *when hoes want it all, but can't handle the piece they get.*

No man asks me questions, and I don't answer any. My biggest pet peeve is when women can't control their men. They think a girl like me should take up the job and do it for them. First of all, I don't accept applications to train a man on being a good boy. He's grown, and so am I. She will either get with the program or roll by it. Second, I don't fuss with females, and I won't talk much either. After making my case known, I'm aiming at the bowl that holds her thoughts and that hole under her nose.

So, don't think I'm not plotting on you when you walk up, because I am. One can say being five foot one and weighing one hundred and fifty pounds, you must have a back-up weapon. People think I can't throw these hands because of my kid-like size. That is their mistake. At an early age, I had to defend myself, so I took up karate as one back-up. Although I don't throw my weight around, I know what I can do when the time comes.

Last, every girl has a homegirl, and every man has a homie. As for me, my ride-or-die bestie is Beast. He is my real road dog, because if I holler a command, my blue faithful friend is taking whoever it is out. Snickering at the event that just unfolded, I drove as the evening air felt right on my body. I looked over at Beast and his head was out the window, letting the breeze blow upon his face.

I took Beast to the house and put him up. I'm so glad we live in the country, because the city has too many regulations for dogs and parties. Realizing I was late for work, I showered and got dressed in a hurry. Using the phone, I let Jarissa know I was on my way, so she could let my captain know. Soon as I got dressed, I grabbed my headphones and put on my hype music. To work on this job, you must have build-up music. You can't go on this job and not have Boosie, Gotti or Jeezy blaring from your vehicle or headphones. Every day, I play "Bulletproof" by Gotti, it's my song.

If you don't hype up, your day will be a drag, and you won't enjoy your job; that's why I get hyped and ready. Mainly, it's the people I work with that make the job worthwhile. We're all like family, take up for each other, and hang out together in some form. Here, it isn't about the money. If it were, I would've quit before I got started. The pay on a regular scale would suck, but I'm one of the highest paid because I have a doctorate in criminal justice and Drug Tactics, with emphasis on the K-9 unit. Therefore, money isn't an option and a job isn't either.

Arriving at work, I looked around before I went in the building. To the left is the County PD, the jail is in the middle and the City PD is on the right. I grinned because the way this building is set up, we all meet in the middle and that is funny to me. Parking around back with a hop in my step, I got out my truck. Bell met me at the door, with his usual smile.

"What is it?"

He shook his head. I knew it must be something because of the way he stared as he smiled with his fine ass. *I should have been fucking him when his wife thought I was, but that's water under the bridge.* Placing my headphones back on

15

my head, I went in the building. I gave Renee a "what's up" nod as I danced my way towards the bathroom. Once I checked my look in the mirror, I thought, *if it weren't for me getting my heart broke by Ve-Lo; I never would've joined the girls in blue.*

My badge caught my eye because I take pride in wearing this golden star. However, it worked out better for me. I'm now a real bitch and have a pointy item, which says I'm legal with it. Jailer Jarissa Parks came in. I smiled because she is a hustler for real and has been a smooth talker all her life. I say she is the finest of the girls in blue. She is Scott County bred. All the way from Sebastopol Elementary School throughout high school, she was smart and would've gone further, but she came back home years ago, pregnant.

That pregnancy gave way for her staying in the county and having another child, which landed her this job. I must admit, in a brief time she became the top jailer. She's in her element here, everyone knows her, and everyone wants her on their team. She has the streets on lock and God knows who else on her side. Not only is she popular, but she is the gamer above all gamers. Jarissa is also my best friend and one of my beloved cousins. She knows every scheme there is and then some. If it can't be done, it's because she hasn't done it.

She has all the inside information on anything and everything. It's like she's on both sides of the law. Seeing her made me stop my music as I took off the headphones. She stood at the door and said quietly, but in suspense, "Girl. What the hell happened at the car wash on Northside today?"

Smiling, I dropped my head some and shook it a few times. I knew then Texan's girl had been here. *That sneaky bitch,* I thought as my mouth said, "You know Texan from the tracks?"

"Yeah, what about his nickel and dime ass?"

"Today he let one of his hoes get out of line. So, I politely put her back in her place."

"Well, you in trouble. Captain is hot and is waiting on you in her office."

Turning my head, I replied, "I'll bypass her office and go straight outside. She won't even know I came in until she leaves."

Shaking her head no, she replied, "No way, she has the door open and told us if she misses you, we better direct you, her way."

"Damn, thanks for the heads up."

"Bet."

Jarissa eased out the door as I finished fixing my clothes. Soon as I walked out, Captain was standing in the doorway, and she was not too pleased. I said, "Hello," as if I didn't know.

"In my office now!"

CHAPTER 2

Captain went in first and sat at her desk. I walked in without shutting the door. With a frown, she said, "Close the door, Cat."

She called me Cat, which meant she is truly angry, and my talk must be extremely slick. I closed the door and sat down. She stared at me. I asked, "What?"

"You know what."

"No, I don't."

"You mean Jarissa didn't warn you?"

Giving her my usual coy smile, I said shyly as I burst out, "Yeah, she did. But let me explain."

"Please do."

"Beast and I were at the Northside car wash. She was in a yellow Nissan, and she came at me, advising me to stay away from Texan, a lame that can't hold onto his money."

"She said you hit her, choked her and squeezed her throat. I persuaded her not to file charges on you. I told her I would talk to you about the matter."

"So? I was wrong. She had two other tall women with her. How did I know they wouldn't do anything?"

She sat up and began messing with papers on her desk as she spoke, "You have a badge."

"One I'm proud of."

She stopped moving papers around and spoke professionally. "Your top job is to protect and serve the people; not make them fearful of you. Even if you didn't know what her actions were; you knew it and you struck first." Sighing, she said loud enough for me, "Desk duty for one week."

"You serious?"

With her usual look, she started back moving the papers on her desk. "Yeah, and it starts in the morning. So, go home and be prepared to start at six am and leave at six pm."

I jumped up and placed my hands on her desk. "Come on, Captain. You know you need me on the streets. I can't do anything behind a desk, filing papers and watching all the action going off without me."

"I do, but you too 'bout it out there. Maybe this will cool you down."

I removed my hands and stood up, speaking innocently, "Ma."

"Don't 'Ma' me. You should be glad I don't transfer you out. You have so many complaints on you. The average captain would not think twice about sending you to another department, Cathy. Daughter, you live like you are invincible and with your hardcore attitude, you act as if you are off limits and can't be touched by anyone, including me. "

20

"I'm the entire package, Ma, but I do my job. I'm one, if not the best police officer you have here, and it's not because you, my momma. It's because I get the job done and I make the people feel safe when they obey the law."

"For those that isn't afraid of you, and I wonder how much of the county is that?"

"Ma, regardless of what the majority of people think; I get results because I'm just that good. When we say show hands, they should obey and show their hands and not ask us questions we don't have to answer. We are the police, and we are the law of the land. My job requires making those that abide the law safe, and I do just that; whether the other half of the county likes it or not."

"You are one of my top, if not my best police officers, but you can be hazardous here. I can't afford a liability here either. Daughter, cool off. The people already don't trust us, and we must earn their trust and vice versa."

"Alright, I will calm down, but don't think she's not gonna pay for getting me in trouble over dick I haven't gotten in a while."

"Cat, you haven't left my office yet and you already talking about making her pay."

"All I'm saying is, she started it, and I'll show her how to play it the way it should be played. I'll be nice and I promise, I won't cause any havoc."

She pointed towards the door and said sternly, "Go, Catherine."

I walked out her office and closed the door. Soon as I turned around, some of my fellow workers were laughing at me. One even threw a wadded-up paper at me as I spoke, "Funny."

Jackson came my way and pretended to look down at the papers as he stood by me in a joking manner. I knew something was up as he asked, "Cat, I have some reports. Could you go file them for me, ASAP? I'm on the night shift and a call; you know, kick in a door or two, handcuff some folks and write tickets, you know real work like that."

They all laughed as I playfully swung at him. Observing the people in the medium office, I asked, "So, you all think this is cute that I'm on desk duty?"

They mumbled amongst themselves as I heard, "I don't think it's cute."

I looked at the door and it was Bell. I expected a smart remark as I asked with my hands on my hips, "Why isn't it cute?"

"You crucial in the field and they don't expect the County PD to have our own short fuse dynamite that blows without striking the stem. Come on, you can't beat that."

As I held up one finger, I asked, "See, I have one fan. Can I get two? Can I get two people that don't think desk duty is cute?"

"I'm your fan," Dispatcher Renee Parks-Butler agreed with humor as she stood in the door.

We laughed and when Captain Le Beau opened the door, they all started walking off. Soon as she closed the door, we snickered. I left out and headed home with sleeping with Texan on my mind. Other than that, I would've left him alone for good. She threw the first punch, but when I punch back, it will hurt and hit her hard.

Getting angrier thinking of what she did, it made me call him and set something up. He answered and I told him I will get at him later and he was happy. I got home and fed Beast. Soon as Beast finished eating, I let him walk around the yard. I was already bored, and then I heard all the fun Bell and Jackson was having on the scanner. Knowing 5am come quick. Unlocking the door, turning off the alarm and locking the door back, I stripped and got in the bed.

The next morning, I arrived at work and the day shift workers greeted me, but they aren't the ones I'm used to. They

23

showed me the reserved desk, and I plopped down, feeling lost. Another three hours passed and still there was nothing. I don't see how day shift does this all day for a living. I saw Jarissa, but she was busy, so I went back to the countryside.

For almost another three hours, nothing happened. No one came in with complaints. I didn't have a call at all. *At night, we kick in doors and make house calls. It's never boring, it's exciting,* I thought as I hyped myself up by playing my music and dancing with my headphones on. I'm not careless because with every call, you never know what to expect. But here on day shift, it is quiet, relaxed, and laidback. To know I'd be here for a whole week didn't make me anxious.

I gave dispatchers breaks and while they were out, I didn't even get a disturbance call. Not even a call for a car dying. The usually rowdy hood didn't have anything happening. I couldn't believe I was on day shift and not at home, sleeping from a long night of arresting people. Captain came out her office. I pulled my headphones off to shake my head no. She knows I don't like sitting in one spot. I guess all my moving around made her think I have ADHD. She laughed at me. She knows I'm bored out my mind and I work best in a patrol car. I asked, "Will it get better than this?"

"Who knows?"

"It has to. I have a week here and if the first day is the impression of how the rest is, I'm in trouble."

Captain smiled and said, "I'm enjoying this too much. At least, I know you are safe."

"This isn't a safe job. If I wanted safe, I would've chosen another profession."

"If you weren't so much like your father, I wouldn't have to put my foot down but Cat, when you get hyped up on Mountain Dew and that music; you a piece of work."

"Put your foot down next week; let me get back on night shift this week."

My mother, the captain, laughed. I knew she wasn't budging. I must admire my mother. She raised me by herself, after my father was killed in the line of duty when I was seven. That was about eighteen years ago; since then, we have been close. She wants me settled down with a child or two, but like I told her, I haven't met the one yet who could contain me and my ways. She stopped pressuring me when she became my boss. Now, she is on me like sin on a sinner.

Stuff you would think I could get away with, I couldn't with her. She doesn't cut me slack, child or not. Her nieces, Jarissa and Renee both work here and they stay out of her way. Not me. As soon as six pm hits, the shift was over, and I clocked out. Captain was already gone and so was Renee. I went outside and was almost in my truck when Jarissa came over. She stood in the door and stated in a happy tone, "How you like being in the building all day, Cat?"

I rolled my eyes with disgust as I got out and placed myself beside her. I shook my head no and said, "Girl, I don't see how y'all do this. This is beyond me. I felt like a caged animal that was bored out of its fucking mind. Nothing happened; not even a disturbance call or a routine traffic check. Now I know why all of day shift is sorry and fat."

We laughed because they all are somewhat overweight, and I believe it's the lack of calls that comes in. Jarissa said, with some type of comfort, "It's not that bad. You see, in here is where you hear everything."

"Well, out here is where you see everything." We laughed more as I stated, "I have a week of this. God help me."

"Thank God it wasn't two weeks and look on the bright side, at least you'll be safe."

"Life isn't safe. Momma said the same thing. Jarissa, you will either be active or passive in your life; the choice is yours. Believe me, I don't intend for my life to happen, and I don't have anything to say about it."

"Girl, the word on the inside is we getting a new investigator on Monday."

"What about the other one?"

"You mean the one I was sleeping with?"

"Yeah, the one you copied evidence keys from; yeah, him."

She laughed as she spoke casually, "He signed up and got deployed for another tour of duty. But, before he left, he was acting all weird."

"Sure, the hell was."

"He might have been crazy, but his money was some kind of stupid and all the dope I wanted. Do you hear me?"

I laughed as she said more. "He was older, but I didn't do without anything. My kids went anywhere, and we did anything we wanted, because of his middle class, lonely ass."

"He probably got broke fucking off with you."

"That ain't my problem. I think the new investigator is Bell's brother-in-law; the one I talked on the phone with about Christ and church. But I'm not sure if he accepted the job. He came highly recommended, and I won't know until a little later."

"If it's someone you had conversations with, he better not be like the last guy that left."

"Not like that. Cooley was and is more like a confidant than anything else; then again, somebody else says it's not him but someone else from another department."

27

Knowing her choice in men, the statement came out, "I can imagine your taste, but what else they say?"

"I have wonderful taste, thank you. If it's not Bell's brother-in-law, they say the other guy is strictly by the book's kind of guy."

"Another hard ass?"

"Yup and worse than the one that just left; per the word on the inside."

"Where they pick these men at?"

"I don't know, but this one; they say he gets results, but not as much as Cooley. Besides, I don't know why he would want here. He is overqualified and could be a captain somewhere else. They also said Te-Te may retire next year."

"How the hell you hear all that? I'm her daughter and I haven't heard it."

"Like I said, Cat, inside is where you hear everything."

"Are any of these men married?"

"No, but Bell's brother-in-law has a son."

"See, that's the problem. They hire men that are hard up and don't have a life. The majority make their co-workers miserable. I don't like being careful about talking in front of someone. If I must watch you like that, it's best if we don't speak at all."

"I feel you on that, but Bell's brother-in-law is the one we hope to get. I know he is nice and can be something serious if pissed off, among other things."

"Other things like what?"

"All I know is, he doesn't socialize like we all do. He does his job and doesn't really talk, until you know him; and then it's about church and serving the Lord."

"Has any of his 'church' talking done any help for you?"

"Yes and no."

We started laughing as I stated, "Wow. Where he from, then? Hell?"

We chuckled more as Jarissa said, "Nah. He from Florida or Georgia, somewhere in the South. I can't remember."

"Hell, we live in the South."

Giving me a playful push, she said, "South, but on the east side of the United States."

"That's more like it but, I wonder why Forest?"

"Beats the hell out of me; can't be for the money unless he has a degree. He's kind of like you, Cat."

"Like me? You tell those ear hustling fuckers to keep their mouths off me. They can't do them if they are keeping up with me and the stuff I do."

29

CHAPTER 3

We laughed, but if I know Jarissa like I do, she will tell them just what I said. I asked, "What about the other guy?"

"I hadn't heard anything really on him, but he's worse than Bell's brother-in-law."

"Ok, so what you got up for this Saturday night? It's been a minute since we partied."

"Hold on a minute," Jarissa stated as she looked at her text.

"It's official, we all gathering at Bell's house for a party."

"For what?"

She kind of squeezed her eyes as she spoke, "For the new guy."

"So, they did pick him?"

"Yeah, someone sent me a confirmation. He is so fine and sweet, and he is the kind of man a woman needs in her life."

"Go for it."

"Nah, he encourages me, but I wouldn't mind."

"Sounds like it's more than that."

"It isn't, but he's too slow for me."

"But he is single."

"I know and that makes him unattractive, because I like taken men, and the party will be full of them. The question is, are you going?"

"Hell yeah, how many people you know turn down free food and drinks?"

"Right," my girl added.

"Then again, I might come if Bell asks me."

Jarissa looked me up and down as she spoke. "When have you ever asked for permission about somewhere that included someone wearing blue?"

"True, but I don't care for his wife."

"What's she done?"

"Have you forgotten when she was just dating Bell, she accused him and me of fucking, with no real proof?"

"Sure, the hell did," Jarissa spoke as she looked like she forgot.

"He told me she gets mad listening about how he talks about the job. She's forgotten I work close with her husband and quite naturally, if he discusses his job, my name will come up."

"If I were her, I would look at you too, because you always into something. And to know her husband works with you closely, that's reason enough to watch your suspect ass."

"She better keep what part of him she already has. Truthfully, we work together, and he makes me laugh. He isn't my type."

"And your type is what, Cat? No one really knows what your type is. I'm your family and I'll just be guessing."

I grinned hard before saying, "Don't know, ain't really been looking for a type, when I can get licked when I want and get money when I want. I'm about taking that bread and being eaten like bread on a sandwich."

"Don't ever mix business with pleasure. Believe me, it's not worth it."

"I know; that is one reason why I don't date friends."

We laughed a few more moments, then I said, "Hit me up later. I'm going home."

"I get off in another hour, come over and chill."

"Bet."

"Bet."

I got in my truck and locked down, turned up the tunes and began driving. I took the route by Gaddis Park. A few seconds later, blue lights were flashing in my rearview mirror. Signaling, I pulled over to the right by the basketball court. A county cop pulled up close behind me, while another county cop car pulled up in an angle and blocked me in. I turned down the tunes because I'm being stopped. We county cops don't ever stop someone in the city, unless it is a noticeable violation, and violations must be addressed.

However, this county cop in front of me stated on the bullhorn, "Little child, get out the truck with your hands up."

Little child? I thought, as I didn't see who it was. Whoever he was, he was by the car as I replayed his voice. I opened the door and jumped out my truck with my hands up in a "what you want" stance. Then I heard, "Oh, it's Hell Cat."

I spoke with humor, "You knew who I was, while ya playing; talking about a little child."

It was Bell and Jackson, the pranksters of the county department. I was laughing as I asked, "What y'all stopping me for? While ya wasting my time and money."

"Someone reported that a child was driving a grown folk vehicle, and they can't see over the steering wheel."

"Cute, but you don't have anything better than wasting taxpayer's money?"

"Trust me, at night we earn every bit of the taxpayer's money," Jackson said.

Bell walked closer from behind and asked, "Cat, you coming Saturday? We having a party at my house for my brother-in-law. You know he's joining the force as an investigator."

"I just heard."

"Jarissa just now telling you?" he asked with a smile.

"She been busy and she got at me when I was getting in my truck. I'll be there and what kind of music y'all playing? I don't feel blues all the time. I can't get hype."

Jackson said, "You may not want her hyped, Bell. We don't want our dynamite blowing up for nothing."

He laughed and Bell said, "I can arrange that. I'm the DJ for the night."

"Bell, you can't do a lot of things and DJ'ing is one of them," I stated to my co-worker.

"I see there are some things about me you have forgotten."

"She too busy beating people up with her dog at North-Side car wash," Jackson said in a funny way.

I faced him and said, "No, I'm not beating people up, they front with their girls and get mad when I call 'em out."

Bell said, "Let's go, Jackson, this little girl has to get home. We have grown folk work going on tonight."

They all walked off as I spoke, "I will be on night shift soon."

"Yeah, in a full week."

"Ha-ha, don't get everybody, save me some."

They laughed and pulled off. How I have fun with them. It is a joy working with men like that. They have my back, and I have theirs. We always do something as a team because we are a family. We all know a lot about each other, and we all help each other out because we close. It feels good to have brothers, even if they are not blood related.

Soon as I arrived at Northside Store on Highway 35, I saw Texan and his girl. She gave me a fake grin. Being who I am, I walked over. Texan was watching as I spoke, "You went to my job and told my captain on me?"

"You hit me, and I should have filed charges and the next time you do, I will."

"Because you went on my job, I will catch you low and make your tattle tale ass pay."

"Like I said, you touch me again, I will press charges on yo short midget ass."

"You gonna press something and charges won't be it."

Walking off from her, I paid for my gas and went to pump it. I was going to order a pizza but decided against it since I was almost at home. She came out the store and left with Texan. Replacing the pump, I got back in my truck. Before I could make it in the driveway, my cell went off. It was Texan. Pretending to be angry, I spoke, "What is it?"

"You busy?"

"I'm too busy for bullshit. Don't you have yo hoe wit you?"

"I just took her home."

"Ok, what's up?"

"I saw you in uniform and couldn't resist you. Let me come over."

"Ok, come over. Give me about thirty minutes, but you only have ten minutes, and you better have some money."

I got home and parked my truck in front of my two-bedroom, two-bath log cabin. I went around back and opened the shed door for Beast. Soon as I put the meat in his big pan, he started eating the dripping blood-red steak like no problem. That's right; I feed him blood so he will be crazy. For a few minutes, I watched him eat and drink his water. Once he was finished, I unhooked him. My entire property is fenced in for Beast to parade around.

He is my guard, and I haven't had any intruders or an attempt. I do have "Beware of the dog" signs up only because I have to. Although, on the days the electric company comes, I'm here or I tie him up for a few days. I unlocked the door to step in and locked the door back. I checked my house out and it was still intact. Going straight to the bathroom, I knew I had to wash off and smell good. It's not that I stink but being with a man I must smell cleaner and fresher.

I just hope he isn't sloppy this time. I can't stand a man who does a sloppy job when he pleases me. *What a complete turn off,* I thought. Putting on a sexy gown, I turned the automatic heat up. I texted Captain and asked:

Me: *What you cooking today?*

Cap: *You cook*

Me: *I'm coming over in an hour.*

Cap: *You will just be coming over.*

No eating Mom's cooking today, I thought. I didn't text back as I put my phone on vibrate. In a way, that is an advantage of having a parent close by.

But it is annoying when they come over unannounced. With my mom, I don't worry about that; she was seeing some school superintendent. *Now that is a career change for real,* I thought as I heard a horn blow. Peeping out the window, I saw it was Texan. I called out, "Stand down" and Beast did as he was ordered, by going into an at-ease stance. Texan acted like he didn't know where his car went as I yelled out, "One minute."

I put on my house shoes and went outside. I don't ever take men in my house because it is my house. We always use a hotel or their ride. Tonight, I didn't feel like driving to Carthage for him to please me. Opening his car door, I got in and the first thing I said was, "That bitch of yours went on my job and got me in trouble."

He grinned as he spoke plainly, "She told me. I told her to stay away from you."

"Don't worry about it. I have something for her when I catch her off again."

"Cat, she's young and has a few more years on paper."

"I don't give a damn how young she is or what she has on paper. She shouldn't play in a grown woman's world if she's a child."

"Enough talking about her; where my other friend at?"

"Where my money at?" I asked with a sly tease.

Texan reached in his wallet and handed me three hundred dollars. I put the money deep in my pocket. However, that doesn't matter because I recheck my money before I leave wherever I'm at. I reached in my jacket pocket and handed him the box of clear wrapping paper. It's silly, but at least this way, I stay out of relationships and don't get caught up in emotions, as well as staying pleased at the same time.

While Texan was getting things together, he repeated himself. "I saw you today in that uniform and that has been all I could think about. Right now, you smell good and turning me on."

"Well, stop talking about it and get your mouth full. I do have shit to do."

I laughed. Other than his money, he's cool peeps. I met him before he got with the woman he has now. I didn't want a commitment, and she did. He did the right thing by moving her in. But, whenever I want him, he becomes my toy. No matter who he's with, he can't seem to tell me no. Mostly, it isn't easy to find a guy you can get along with. Not just get along with, but one who understands the game you both play by. He does whatever he wants and so do I. We know what we do, and we're grown about it.

Being I'm a step up from the floor, I need a fellow well over six feet. Texan is just that; tall and mine when I want him. I got out the extended cab truck and waited for him. He got out with his shirt off as he let the bed of the truck down. In the back of the truck, he has a soft plush carpet. I could tell it was new as he said, "I had this put in today and you the first and only I want back here."

"Boy, save that for that water-head girl that is gone over you. I'm not the one."

"Cat, you are the one I want."

"Boy, you come out better wanting something else, because this isn't it and I won't be it."

"You do that to a nigga. You bring that emotional shit out of me."

"You going to talk or please? Cuz, I have things to do."

He laughed at me. I don't have all night for him. I'm not romancing him. All he can do is please me and get on 'bout his business. Climbing in the back, I scooted back and opened my legs wide. Seconds later, he began teasing me. I could only stare up at the stars because it was early and I'm going down to Jarissa's in another hour. Closing my eyes, I couldn't get into his sexual foreplay, so I pretended it was too good. He bought it hook, line and sinker. Glancing at him, he asked, "When you gonna let me get it?"

"Get what?"

"The pussy, that's what I'm talking about. It's been a while since I been inside you."

"You haven't been inside me since you got involved in a steady relationship."

"And I miss you every time I'm with her."

"And?"

"And what?"

"And you can keep on missing."

"What is the difference? I please her pussy too."

"Yeah, but you use foil on mine."

I gave him a smirk, laughing; I know lines when I hear them. Not caring I responded, "And you aren't getting in me this evening. I have shit to do."

"It better not be another man pleasing you," he spoke with a serious tone.

I looked at him. He was serious. I thought it was funny. Kindly as ever, I spoke, "It's none of your business if another man is getting it, and if there is or was what the hell can you do about it?"

He didn't say anything. Texan was thinking because he knows he can't do anything about what I do; that is why I'm not in a relationship. I saw he was kind of hurt but I didn't care. Being that he wasn't answering the question, I did it for him and made sure he knew where we going with what we are doing. I was tickled "You aren't doing a damn thing but shutting the hell up and falling back in line. I ain't yours and you damn sure ain't mine. Cut the touchy feelings out before you get your heart broke. Been there, done that."

Texan got up and acted like he was mad. I scooted up and said, "I don't care about you being mad. What the hell does that mean? You know we do what we do, and we get on down. So, whatever it is you feeling, feel it with somebody else, because I hook them in like Kareem and fade away like Jordan."

With sadness in his tone, he replied, "Cat, you are one coldhearted-ass bitch."

"Damn, that shit might be true. I heard that before. But then again, it's me in your face and it doesn't have to be."

"Cat, come on don't do me like that," he said in a begging way.

"Why not? You having sensations and theories about us; that ain't gone be. You will become a problem for me and I'm not trying to get problems. That's for people that can't control their end."

"Will you ever change for a man?"

"Maybe for the right one."

"I'm not the right one?"

I started laughing in his face. "Be for real. You have a woman and you cheating. How the hell can you be the right one for me and you aren't even the right one for her?" He didn't say a word as I spoke, "My thoughts exactly."

CHAPTER 4

Leaving him looking stupid, I went in the house, closed the door and locked it, placing the money on the table. He took off. I went in the bathroom and took another shower. This time, I put on a sweatpants outfit and made Beast wipe his paws on the towel before getting in the truck. I blasted my song and Beast started barking. Letting the windows down, Beast put his head outside as I drove towards Jarissa's house in Lone Pilgrim.

Soon as I passed the church, I turned right. Seconds later, I turned into Jarissa's yard. She was there and so was Renee. Parking the truck around back, I got out. With my roller leash, Beast followed me as I walked up. Tying Beast up, I sat down, and Jarissa handed me a wine cooler. She sipped her drink before asking a stupid question. "You always take that damn dog with you?"

"Say what you want, he is down for me. I give him some orders and I promise you; he follows them better than any man."

My girl laughed and said, "You should have stayed on the K-9 Unit if you like dogs that well."

"Thought about going back, but I like hanging out with you too much for that," I spoke as I started laughing.

"And Renee is a married square. Guess I'm your best bet." Jarissa spoke with humor.

"Maybe you two should get married and find out if I'm a bored, married square. Honestly, you both need the Jesus team and to have a real life."

"I don't know about the Jesus team, but here on earth, I can go and come as I please. That sums it up. I don't think there's an earthly man who can make me change for him."

Jarissa added, "I don't know any man can make you change, Cat. If you change, someone must have died."

"Right, so Renee; you talk that married crap all you want but keep it moving. I'm good on my end. How about you, Jarissa?"

"It's damn good on my end."

Renee chuckled before saying, "Cat, you don't ever know what life will thrust upon us. If the Lord operates in our lives and we're not just living a life; we can find life is worthwhile while we are here on earth with a man."

"My life is worthwhile," I stated at Renee.

"How is that when the Lord isn't involved?"

"Jesus minds *his* business, and I mind mine; it's a win-win situation," I stated as Jarissa agreed by giving me a toast.

"Besides, everyone isn't blessed with a wonderful husband like you, Renee. We push through the scum of the

44

earth or play in somebody else's dirt until we find the kind of ground we are looking for," I said before sipping some more.

Jarissa put her drink down and added, "Cat is right. I've slept with all kinds of men, mainly my favorite kind; the taken kind and still they all are the same. Some would even take off their wedding ring until we finished, then put it back on like they hadn't gotten my goods. I mean, wearing a wedding band doesn't make you faithful, loyalty does."

Renee said, "No, wearing a wedding band isn't about keeping one faithful and I agree. Many men, married too, will and can be the most deceitful ones; that is why you give yourself to Christ. Be married to *him*. *He* will in no ways cast you out and you won't wonder if he is faithful or not. *He* says *he* won't ever leave you nor forsake you like earthly man can do. Who knows, girls, Mr. Right could be around the corner."

"Around the corner for whom? Not me," Jarissa replied, looking around.

I opened another wine cooler before saying, "I don't believe marriage is it for me either. It's too complicated. Too many 'don't do this. Don't do that.' I say Fuck that and do you."

Jarissa laughed as she drank another wine cooler. Renee kept on talking and saying, "Nothing is complicated when Christ is involved in your life. You could see things you never seen before. *He* will be there for you when you feel like there is no one. To follow him and love him is so simple that children understand his word better than adults."

"I can see all those things being single too," I stated as I laughed.

"I feel you on that, Cat. I already have kids, bills and freedom, without the hassle of a husband."

"You two are knocking it without even trying it. I'm saying, let Christ be your husband. Try being married to *him*. Think about it. In earthly terms, no lonely nights, someone that helps pay bills, there for you and so much other good stuff. Just add Christ and see how much sweeter things would be. He said whosoever will let them come. He also says how he stands at the door of your heart knocking. My Lord won't break the door of your heart down, because he wants you to willingly let him in."

"That may be true but with Jesus, you have church all the time, being put in a category about religion, pretending to be something you might not be, and with a man you also have drama, bullshit and did I say bullshit?"

Renee shook her head as we began laughing as Jarissa's two children came outside, yelling excitedly, "Beast, Beast."

Jumping up, I rushed over to stop Beast from reacting. He doesn't play with children, and I don't play with him because if you play with him, he can't do his job. I spoke quickly at Jarissa, "He isn't a child's pet. Tell those chaps of yours to stay the hell back."

She stopped her children and made them go back in the house. However, it never fails, whenever I come over, I have to stop her children from playing with Beast. To change the subject, Renee asked, "So, what you do when you got off from day shift today?"

"I took a bath, got in a sexual relation, made a little extra money, washed back off and came here."

Renee shook her head with a hint of smile before saying, "Cat, you always so blunt. I don't want to hear that. I thought you would've said ate supper and whatever, whatever. That is your personal business, but you talk so casually about it. What you do in your bedroom is on you, but the Word tells you not to defile your marriage bed."

"You know we ain't married, sis," Jarissa said as she drank some more wine.

"Then be careful of the questions you ask people like me if you are not prepared for the answer. There is no shame in my game, because I know my game," I stated.

Jarissa added, "Renee, I could have told you Cat isn't secretive."

"Cat needs my Jesus, and all that kind of talking and premarital things will leave."

"Maybe, but not anytime soon. I'm enjoying me right now," I stated as we drank some more wine coolers.

"You been by your mom's?" Renee asked.

"No, I texted her earlier about cooking and she texted back saying she wasn't cooking. No food ended my dropping by her house."

"Yeah, her fellow over there," Jarissa added.

"I know. That is why I should pop in like she be doing me sometimes when she didn't have a man. I couldn't do anything without the fear of Momma pulling up on me; had me acting like I was six or seven years old again, hiding my life from my mom."

"That is, ya mom," Renee said.

"Yeah, and Ma needs to mind her own business and don't come in my yard, because I don't invite my hoes in my house. She'll come over and see me being naughty."

We started laughing as Jarissa opened a bottle of wine. Renee spoke, "Look, it's been fun but family, please think about what I said. None of us know when our time here is up and we don't want to die not knowing if we know Jesus or not."

"Don't tell that lie. You know it has not been fun," Jarissa said with laughter.

"Sis, it is always good talking with you, even when you don't listen. I love you and I want you to come to church with me this Sunday."

"I have to work," Jarissa said lowly.

"What about you, Cat?"

"Me too. I have work," I lied.

She smiled and said, "I know you lying, but that's ok. You'll come when you've had enough of the way y'all live."

"I don't see how. I love doing me and no man can change that."

"Jesus can and *he* can do so much more for your life if you allow him to. He won't force you, but he will let things happen. Let me go. My husband is home, and I told him I was going to come over and stay a few."

Renee gave us a hug as she left in her car. Jarissa asked, "What you think about what she said?"

"I mean, I say a silent prayer from time to time before I kick a door in or make an arrest."

"She goes overboard when she talks about Jesus and living right. She acts like I like the way I live."

"I don't think that is it. You know ya sis like I know her. She means well and sometimes I take heed of the things

49

she tells me. It's not easy to up and follow Jesus as she says. Renee makes it look so easy, but I don't know. I hadn't been in a church in a long time and the shit I do will get me kicked out of Heaven for sho."

"You don't do half the crap I do. I mean, I feel something when she talks about it, but that feeling goes away as soon as she goes away."

At the end of that sentence, Jarissa got up and checked on her children. I already knew what time it was, and I wasn't comfortable about her, but it's her business. I knew she was rushing Renee off so she could do her. As much as I have seen her do her thang, I should be ok with it, but I wasn't. In fact, it grieves me seeing her do what she does. If there is a God, I hope he delivers my girl before she does some crazy stuff.

I worked around drugs for years and it can wreak havoc on people who love the junk. I have warned her numerous times, but she would not listen. She always says the same ole thing, *I'm grown, and I do what the hell I want*. She is right so I keep my opinions to myself, although I still tell her the truth, even if she doesn't like it. Her easing the door shut, made me look up. She sat in her usual spot. Clearing off a spot on the glass table, she took out the small container.

I took another swallow of wine while I watch her position herself closer to the table with her head going in for a nosedive. She perched herself on the edge of the chair and she shook some. Jarissa made the familiar white trail on the table. She got her thin coffee straw from inside the tin container. Turning my head towards Beast, I heard her sniffing. When she stopped, I faced her. My cousin's eyes were closed as she held her head back so the thin powdered drug could its way towards her brain.

I remembered *I told her I would rather be an occasion drinker because cocaine, meth, heroin and weed are not my ideal drugs. I would tell her about the effects of the drug, but we'd only get into it. You get tired of seeing your best friend cutting her life short and being addicted on a powerful drug. I reminded her how various people make the drug different, and she doesn't need to get her drugs from all around the world; but she doesn't hear me. She is so content on living her life her way and that is fine, but Renee talking about Christ has planted a seed in me.*

However, it is her life, and I feel helpless about it. I'm not a snitch, but sometimes I wish I were just so she can get help. It aches my core how strung out she is becoming on pure 'caine. I got on her case when she was on meth and popping pills. I thought she had stopped because she was her old self again, but she hadn't. Jarissa just got smarter about how and when; that's how she fooled me and everyone else on the job.

Just like any other person addicted to drugs, they don't think they have a problem, and I can't convince her otherwise. I was devastated when I found out nothing has changed for her. She had been doing cocaine and God knows what, ever since she started messing off with the last investigator. I heard some say he was on powder; they both are and bad. I was just pissed; he knew she would try it because he snorted off and on. Soon as she got hooked, he let her sample all types of 'drugs in the evidence room.

I fear her drug addiction has gotten worse. Sometimes, I see her sniffing as if her nose was running. There have been instances I have found her always touching her nose, shaking, acting nervous, wearing longer shirts to work; I assumed to hide needle marks. It had been rumored she was snorting every day on the job multiple times. I have personally seen her shoot up as we hang out, but it was a while back. I don't want her in trouble, but I want to save her life.

On the other hand, I love her dearly and I know there isn't anything she wouldn't do for me and me for her; that is also why I don't tell her anything anymore. A crack head could sell you out not caring about what they have done because of their obsession. She is lucky my mom tells us when the drug testing happens so she can get her system clean; if not, she would've been fired a long time ago. When she and I do talk,

Jarissa tells me that getting clean and staying straight is very hard. I can only imagine what her body does when she denies it the want it craves.

Breaking my thoughts, was the sound of her snorting harder again. I glanced at her, and she looked from side to side as if someone was making her afraid. She was acting like a schizo off their meds. I was looking and wondering what was wrong with her. Instantly, her head moved nervously, and her body shook horribly. Jarissa glanced at me and suddenly her head dropped. Jumping up, I yelled out, "Girl, you alright? Jarissa, you alright?"

Picking her head up, she grinned at me in her high state and spoke. "This shit is fucking good. I ain't ever had a line like that."

I sat back down. "Girl, you done blew my high. Where you get that mess from?"

"Texan."

Immediately, I was puzzled and asked, "Why you buying your dope from him? You know his dope ain't that straight. Ain't no telling where he gets it from and who is putting stuff in it. You know better than that."

"The old investigator told me that Texan's cocaine is trash sometimes and he didn't lie, but tonight, it was damn good."

"You don't steal it from the evidence room anymore?"

"When I can't get it from there, I buy it from him and it isn't cheap, especially if it's not good. If your body gets past the first hit of this 'caine, the second hit is easier. Cat, don't you ever get on this drug," Jarissa said as she laid with her head held back.

"You don't have to worry about that."

"I'm serious."

"I know you are, and so am I."

Jarissa sat up and spoke clearly as if she was warning me. "This stuff will make you do stuff you never thought you would do and not only that, you can lose what is important. I can say this because I know I'm a drug addict and my body yearn for drugs of all kinds. It's a high, a rush, I can't explain. I'm not proud of things I've done, but I can't change it. I could check out this Jesus, Renee been talking about. Something must give for me. I can't raise my children like this, and they can't see me or catch me like this. They should have a mother they are proud of and not a druggie like me."

"They are proud of you. Jarissa, just make up your mind and do what you have to. Maybe we both could check out this Jesus thing," I concluded. She laid her head back where she was sitting and closed her eyes again. I know she is in her mood, and I really didn't care, but she is killing herself and I will address her later. "I been thinking about what you said about Bell's brother-in-law."

"What about it?"

"Do they get along?"

"They ok, but they are different in a huge way. Bell is funny and a joker. You can't help but to want him; on the other hand, his brother-in-law is serious, fine, someone that is more settled."

She got herself together as she sat up. Jarissa began to make another line on the table. I looked on in disbelief. *She just talked all about trying Jesus and here she goes again.* My cousin is no better than other people on drugs. They say all kinds of things and when they are doing better, it's back to the same thing. This time I sat and watched her and when she came up for air, she said, "You remember when we were younger, and you wouldn't go anywhere without your teddy bear? I had to tuck you in so you could feel like you were at home when you stayed at our house."

I laughed and said, "Hell yeah. Those were the good ole days, weren't they?"

"Cat, sometimes I sit back and think about my life and all I've been through. Out of all of it, you have been my ride or die. I don't want anything coming between us. I mean, you are closer to me than I am to Renee, my own sister. You understand me and I love you, cuz, for that. I hope you see me get off this and back to my old self. I tell my kids all the time about saying no to drugs, but here I am, doing the opposite."

"You must be high. You back in our childhood and you talking about doing right."

"I am though. I'm pretty fucked up right about now and shit; I'm just recalling things," Jarissa spoke as she coughed.

I laughed as she said, "But, back then I was happier and if I could redo a lot of things, I promise you, drugs and other stuff wouldn't be one of it."

"That goes for a lot of us."

"I don't think you've had it as bad as I have."

"I might not have, but my life is far from perfect, and I know it. What is simple to you might be harder for me, and what is simple to me might be harder for you. We each approaches life and choices differently. We can say we wouldn't do this or that, but would we? We can only hope, and hope is all we have."

"Look at you, sounding like Renee. You sure y'all not sisters and I'm the cousin."

I laughed as my cousin made another small line and I frowned again. My best friend was getting too high for me. I got up and said, "Goodbye, girl."

"No, it's see you later. I don't like saying goodbyes and you know it."

I gave her a hug and spoke, "Ok. You right, see you later." Getting Beast, we rolled out.

CHAPTER 5

Soon as I let Beast roam the yard, I called Texan. He said, "If it isn't my number one girl in blue."

"I'm not your girl but if I were, you would be maggot food by now."

"I see you have attitude to what do I owe the pleasure?"

"You don't need to sell Jarissa a damn thing else. I know like you know that your product isn't worth it."

He laughed, saying, "Does she know you calling me and making demands on her behalf?"

"I don't give a damn what she knows or don't know. If you keep selling it to her, I'm coming for you, and you won't like it when I bring it."

"Is that a threat coming from a girl in blue?" Texan teased.

"Grown women don't make threats, they make promises. And I promise, I will repay you for old and new."

"It means that much to you?"

"It does."

"If she doesn't come again, fine. I'll try. But, if ya girl wasn't so strung out; she could leave it alone, but she too far gone. She ain't the girl you know, Cat. Jarissa is way out in left field for you and me," he spoke with real compassion.

"Well, bring her ass back to the sideline and don't sell her shit. I don't care how much money she has or what she can offer."

"I don't give a damn about what she can offer. I don't want her ass. All I want is her paper."

"And her paper will put you on paper."

I hung up, unlocked the door, reset the alarm and went to bed. The next morning, no sooner than I arrived, I saw Jarissa. She was standing by the door waiting. I got out and she began walking towards me. I thought she was going to tell me about Texan, but I heard her husky voice say, "You will never guess who was in jail and got bonded out the other morning?"

She has now piqued my curiosity as I questioned, "Who?"

"Texan's ole girl."

"No, she didn't."

"Yup, she was in jail."

"What she go for?"

"She had a gun with her, and you know she is a convicted felon on paper."

"Oh wow. Who made the stop?"

"I believe someone on day shift did. She went through a routine traffic stop and they smelled weed."

"Stupid."

Jarissa gave me a nudge and spoke. "Guess God has your back."

"Yeah, he beat me to it."

"You will be at the party tomorrow night for Bell's brother-in-law?"

"Yeah, if I can survive day shift, but what is his name?"

"Wheaton Cooley."

"Sounds like a white man's name."

"Hell, your last name sounds French, which you got from yo daddy. By looking at you, we all know the only French in you is when you get dick in you overseas."

She thought it was funny as she held her stomach laughing. Seeing she was delighting herself in the joke, I asked, "You finished?"

"Wait," she laughed more and more before she stood up and said, "Now I'm finished." She started laughing again as she tried to say, "Girl today is Friday and it goes by so fast, your head will swim."

"I hope so. I wouldn't mind getting drunk tonight."

We went inside and I clocked in and started typing reports. Some of them I wasn't familiar with and some of them were boring; however, it did keep me busy. Before long, I was on lunch break and many people were going to jail. I can say it was busy and six pm came quickly as my girl and I clocked out together.

"What you getting into, tonight?" Jarissa asked.

"Nothing. I'm 10-7 for the weekend, plus it's been a long week. I tell, you night shift is never boring, and the days go by so fast."

"You going off duty for the weekend? How the hell you swing that?"

"I was on day shift all this week, so Captain gave me my days, which fell on the weekend."

"You lucky. I tried getting off, but we can't get people to stay. They start working here being a jailer, then they quit. The money is good, and the job isn't bad."

"Speak for yourself, your job sucks. You always in the building unless you do transport duty; how cool is that?"

We laughed as I asked, "What you doing for the weekend?"

"I'm 10-7 for Saturday and 10-8 on Sunday."

"At least your 10-7 puts you off duty for tomorrow."

"What good is being off on Saturday and reporting in on a Sunday morning? I might want to get fucked up but can't, because I'm back in here."

"What about your kids?"

"They will be at their dad's parents' house for the weekend."

"How they doing since their dad's conviction?"

"They good. It ain't like he has done a lot for them, plus they small."

"Ok. I guess I will head out. I know Beast is hungry, so I'll feed him before we do nose tactics."

"What the hell is that?"

"I put on my arm guard and let him attack it. That sharpens his nose, and he practices attacking individuals with drugs or running from the police."

"Girl, I swear you should work for K-9, I ain't lying."

"If you leave, I'll leave."

"Ok. That is what we'll do."

"Let me go because you high on the job, talking about leaving your job."

I laughed at her and drove off. As soon as I made it home, I fed Beast and headed inside. It hit me that I didn't turn on the alarm when I went to work, because it didn't make a noise when I come in. Locking the door and resetting it, I showered, ate and watched *Criminal Minds* and *Law & Order* until sleep came.

The next morning, I ate some cereal and fed Beast before doing a few arm exercises. He was on point, if not better than ever. Beast was proving himself over and over how professionally trained he is. My best friend always does his job and for that, I'm eternally grateful because if he does his job, I can do mine. After working out with Beast for hours, time was getting by, and I was ready. With nothing in mind planned, I wore my hair down. Searching through my closet, I picked out a pair of navy-blue capris, with a white striped top, and blue sandals to secure my feet.

While I was setting the alarm, I heard Beast barking. I know he wants to go. I figured, why the hell not? Quickly, I untied him, and he got on the back of my truck. Leaving out the driveway, I turned right and there at Highway 35's four-way stop was a roadblock. *Damn, I didn't have my seat belt on and they could hassle me,* I thought until I saw the trooper conducting the check and he saw me. I don't know who he is, but he's always smiling at me. It gives me the creeps, because he's married. I don't have time in my life for the shit he could bring just by messing off with him. He waved at me, and I pulled over. I know he doesn't have anything on me other than the seat belt, so I waited. Seconds later, he came over and stated, "I saw you didn't have your belt on, Cat."

"I know. I didn't feel like putting it on, since I'm going two miles from my house."

"You know most wrecks happen close by. I'm just messing with ya, but I do need some play."

"Hell, fuck no. You married."

"It ain't like I could be when I'm with you."

"If you know what is best for you, you will stay in your home, because mine will get you fucked up and put out."

"I like you, Officer Le Beau."

"What's not to like?"

He grinned and asked, "Where you off to?"

"My co-workers are having a party for our new investigator."

"You mean Cooley?"

"I don't know who he is."

"Yeah, it's Cooley. He's a good guy, a good friend of mine that gets results. In fact, I talked with him the other day and he told me he'll be working for the county. I told him he better watch you, because you are a handful. He just laughed."

"That's nice and all, but I have things to do and you stopping me from doing it."

He laughed as he said, "Don't get drunk. If you do, I'll drive you home."

"Good night, Officer."

"Good night, Cat."

He laughed and waved goodbye. I pulled back onto the highway and went towards Scott Central School. I passed Gum Springs Road and seconds later, I arrived at Officer Bell's house. It seemed like a packed house with decorations everywhere. Finally, I parked. I got Beast out and we walked up. Jarissa was already there, along with my other co-workers. There were a few people there I didn't know, but that was fine. Bell came over and said, "I knew you would bring Beast."

"Why wouldn't I? He's my best friend and my protector."

He laughed as I walked behind him. I tied Beast up by Bell's mutts. I didn't like it, but I needed him in an area where they could watch him. Bell shouted, "You ready for a good time!"

"Hell yeah! Bring on the drinks, baby," I screamed out as I came from around back, and a lady came over and handed me a martini with salt dripping around the rim. I tasted it and it was nice. Jarissa came over and I asked, "Where is the guest of honor?"

"He'll be out in a few. Let's party and get fucked up. Before we start drinking, I need a little pick me up."

I looked at her, because I never knew she snorts in public. I said, "You go on and do you, I'm getting my drink on."

65

Jarissa left me and I saw her leaning towards the car. Immediately, I knew I was right. Jackson came over and stated, "Talk to her, Cat."

"You can't tell grown women anything."

"You her best friend."

"I've tried and you know her like I do. She is stubborn and she knows she has a problem. She'll get it together."

"I hope so," Jackson added in a discouraging way.

"At least, I pray she does," I added softly.

Jackson put his hand on my shoulder and spoke to encourage me. "I mean, what we do when we are off duty, you know 10-7; it shouldn't have any consequences, but it does. You know like I know, police and teachers are watched more when we're off the clock than on. We're expected to be saints and not have a life, but that is far from true. We should do us and not be held accountable if we are not breaking the law in public. It's not right or fair to about living an upstanding citizen lifestyle when we should like criminals from time to time; if that is what we want."

"I know and you are right."

"It's not affecting her job performance, but we know firsthand how what crap like that can do and how it can ruin your life; just like that. Just have a talk with her. I don't want her in some mess that could be brewing. She's too good of a person that does an excellent job on the job. Like I said what we do at home is one thing, but she is in public doing her thing. Who says someone here won't notice it or bring her down? We shouldn't know what she does at home, but she is doing it in the public."

"I will talk with her, but right now I'm shaking a leg," I said as I shook my leg with a smile.

"They already short."

We walked in a fast pace back to the party area. I stood by a few other cops as they were exchanging more cop stories than partying. However, that's on them. I danced by myself, having an appropriate time. Jarissa finally came back. When the song went off, I saw her usual glaze and knew she was feeling good.

This young city cop asked for a dance. I figured why not; his dad is mayor of Newton. He was all on me and I kept backing up. It seems the more I backed up, the closer he come. I can't cause a scene, but this pissy boy is working on one. I guess people think because I'm small and party when I can, that means I'm cheap, but I don't sell my body like that and he better chill out before I knock him out.

I was walking off as he grabbed my hand. I looked at him strangely. He asked, "So, you just gonna leave me like that?"

"The song is over and why the hell not?"

"I know you feeling me."

"Feel your hand off my hand."

"I want some of that short ass," he said in a drunken manner.

I didn't say a word. I yanked my hand from his and walked off. If I hadn't walked off, I would fight with him and tonight, it's not about me. I saw Renee under the car porch with the other woman that was either married or old. I screamed out, "Boring."

Renee got up and came to me. She gave me a hug and spoke. "Cat, we being good tonight?"

"If that young punk keeps coming at me, I will give him the business."

"Cat, he's young and fresh out the academy. He's no more than twenty-two."

"And what does that mean? He's still a man in a grown man's world."

"Cat," she said in a warning manner.

"Don't 'Cat' me. Let him do it again, that's all I'm saying and watch what I do."

"Don't do anything I wouldn't do."

"That's easy. You don't do anything."

She smiled and shook her head before asking, "Where's my sis, your ace?"

"She's over there."

"I'm surprised she not over here."

"She doing her thing."

"Oh. I'm leaving. I've been sick all day."

"What's been wrong with you?"

"I don't know. I started having chills and had a slight fever earlier."

"You shouldn't be out here in this cool weather. So, why you come out?"

"We do have a new member of our county family."

"Meeting him isn't that important. It could have waited, if you been feeling sick."

"You know I do my part."

"Have you met him? I mean, is he worth you coming out here sick and all just for him?"

"Yes. He is a very nice man, and he will be attending my church."

"He goes to church. He must be saved."

"He is saved and a father figure for his two-year-old son, which is great. You don't find many men being a good figure like that."

Cutting her off, I stated, "Where is the wife?"

"He is a widower."

Looking at her made me look at him in a different angle. Now, I'm intrigued, but I'll be intrigued later. I smiled at Renee. "Come on. You blowing my high."

"Good. I hope I have blown it all the way home."

She laughed at me and walked back off towards the car porch where the other women were. I danced a few more songs and drank some more. I saw the young boy coming up behind me again. I moved out his way and that didn't work. He still got behind me. I gave Bell my facial expression and he laughed. He knows what I'm thinking, and he knows how I can react in a split second.

The song ended and Bell said on the mike, "Officer Wild Cat, Hell Cat, Tom Cat, or Stray Cat, Cat-period; come center stage. I have a song for you."

I laughed as I yelled back, "I got your Tom Cat."

He said, "Naw, keep that stray in the shelter."

We laughed because we all make jokes and keep it moving. Obeying him, I was on the floor and blasted out Travis Porter's song, "Make it Rain." My hands flew up above my head as my body began to twist slowly as if I were on a pole. Every time I heard, "Make it rain, trick," I placed my hands on the floor and shook my ass for the people. Everyone was around me because they knew I always make the party. The young boy tried to dance with me, and I used him as a prop and danced all around him; not on him, so he couldn't get it twisted. That song was short-lived when Bell said, "Hell Cat, I know you can do better than that. How about this song?"

We all waited on the dance floor until he put on "Ms. Officer," featuring Lil Wayne. My girl jumped in and started dancing with him. I was thankful because I don't need a partner by the way I'm feeling. Soon as the song went off, Jarissa headed towards her car. I looked for Jackson. I know he will be watching her. We make arrests if someone is breaking the law, but when it comes to our own, we watch each other's back. Although she is a jailer, she's in uniform and that still makes her one of us.

Renee came over, said her goodbyes, stopped by her sister and left, headed towards her car. Jackson and his wife were dancing, and I yelled, "You dance better than you patrol."

He yelled back before twirling her, "You dance better on desk duty."

CHAPTER 6

"Ooh, you wrong for that but that's ok, I'm back on the streets come Monday."

"Damn. She coming back."

We laughed as he twirled his wife around again. When we're not talking about the job, he talks consistently about his wife and how he does everything for her and their future. I'm happy for them because Jackson is a great guy. Personally, he gives people too many breaks. I went towards the bar for a Coke and the bartender was sitting as he said, "You been drinking all night. You sure you fit for driving?"

"Are you fit to mind your own fucking business? On this end, I pay my own damn bills."

"People get killed in car wrecks a few feet or a few miles even from their home, and I gather you don't live too far from here."

"What does that have to do with anything? I'm drinking a Coke plain. If I want to drink everything on this bar believe me, I will try."

"Your face don't look happy."

"My face, my business."

"You act like you are unbeatable."

"I been hearing that a lot lately. Thanks, but I came here for a Coke, not Dr. Pibb's advice."

Snatching the Coke, I turned around and that young boy was all in my personal space again. He asked, "You gonna give me some play tonight, because you've been dancing with me and turning me on with those wide hips."

"Boy, turn on a video game and go play. I'm not the game you want tonight."

"You think you better than me because your mom is the captain? I was just sweating you because I hear you sell pussy and I want to buy some, but never mind. There is no telling what you may have."

Forget about this party or the bartender looking on; I lost it and grabbed his small pecan nuts. He fell on the ground on his knees as I squatted with him. Each time he touched me, I squeezed harder and smiled. I looked like he was acting out something, but I knew better. Nicely, I stated, "Now apologize."

The bartender looked on. I guess the rookie has pride, because he didn't say anything. I squeezed a little harder and he shouted, "I'm sorry. Damn, I'm sorry. Let me go."

"The next time I put these young tender nuts in my grasp, I will use my hand as a nutcracker and crack 'em. Is that 10-4?"

He was in tears as he spoke, "Yeah, that's a 10-4."

"Do we have an understanding?" I asked again, causing him more pain.

"Yes, ma'am."

"Now, I'm letting you go, so you can go about your own business and stay out of my business."

When my grip was released, he fell forward. Bell stopped the music and said, "If you fight, there's enough officers here do a J-1 or J-2."

I laughed because I know like he knows; half the police here are either drunk or feeling too good. He spoke, "Since the music is off, let introduce my brother-in-law. He will be working with the best police department in all of Scott County; the County Police Department that is."

The city cops were yelling, "Boo."

One of them screamed, "We demand a recount!"

We laughed as he continued, "City boys don't hate. We kick in doors, and we solve crimes. We get results. You know it like I know it."

The County PD shouted, "Because we do our job, and we get the respect we deserve."

Bell said, "Calm down. My brother-in-law is the reason why we are here this night. He is here all the way from Tampa

Bay, Florida. Let's give a warm Forest, Mississippi welcome to Wheaton Cooley."

They were clapping. I was watching the house for him, but I heard a voice say over my head say, "Excuse me."

I moved out the way and the bartender came through. He is the tallest man I have ever seen. I might have been drinking, but the way those blue jeans hugged his butt; it made me look. He walked towards the DJ stand and turned around. I noticed he is in great shape, very high complexion with a curly fade. Bell gave him the microphone and he said, "Thank you, everyone, for coming out this evening. I was bartending so I could slip in and check you all out. I look forward in this new adventure."

He walked off the platform like it was nothing. From his deep intriguing voice, he sounded like he has an accent or speaks another language. Jarissa walked up, interrupting me, coming from her car. I checked her out and asked, "You feeling good?"

"Girl, I'm higher than a bird in the sky right now."

"Can you drive home? If not stay with me."

"Shid, I'll go home. I'm 10-8 in the morning bright and early."

"It's already one o'clock. I won't be 10-8 'til Monday."

"I will be at work with bells on."

75

"Let's go tell the Scott County Boys bye and I have to get Beast away from those mutts."

We said our goodbyes. I went around back and got Beast. He was alert as usual. With my roller collar in one hand, I led Beast towards the truck. He jumped on back and I got inside, and we left. Sunday morning, I woke up with no hangover. I fed Beast and let him loose. I saw Momma called and we talked for a few while she was on her way to church service. I called Jarissa and she was working and peppy at that. I was glad because last night she was in her car more than usual. That tells me she is hooked deeper. I told her, "When you get off, stop by my place."

"Ok, but can't stay too long. My kids come back by seven this evening."

"It won't take long," I replied.

"Ok."

"What y'all doing at work?"

"Nothing. This is one day I wished I had stayed at home."

"I might swing by, but I don't feel like changing clothes."

"Let me go. It's time for the inmates' last round outside. Later," I heard Jarissa say.

"Later."

I hung up and texted Momma. I told her I was coming by for a few. Putting on some baggy clothes and putting my hair in a ball, I got Beast, and we left for Momma's house without setting the alarm. I called Renee and her husband answered. I told him to let Renee know that I was checking on her and he said he would tell her. No sooner than we arrived, Beast got off the truck and went in his favorite spot. Momma was on the porch and rocking in her chair that Daddy bought her many years ago.

From her character, she is clearly thinking about my dad. She got up and gave me a hug. I sat down and asked, "Why did you hire someone like Cooley? He acts like he is too good for partying with his police family."

"I hired him for you, Catherine."

"What do you mean you hired him for me?"

"He is level-headed, and you run over everyone in the department. I figured, why not give you a challenge since you are a challenge?"

"If you are playing matchmaker, it will not work."

"Daughter, I'm not. You headstrong. Loving someone is something you will do on your own."

"Speaking about love, tell me about your new love interest."

She smiled and I knew she was deep into him, but I haven't met him. Momma touched my hand and said as she stared out towards her driveway, "He isn't your father, but he is so close, it scares me. I never thought I would be feeling like this about another man, but I do. He is a wonderful man and loves me more than I can say. I guess it's just me and how I think things should be."

"Mom, you don't need my approval."

"I know, but you are my only child and what you think means so much."

"You didn't think that way when you put me on desk duty for that week."

She smiled and retorted, "That is business, and this is personal. You are my daughter, and I love you dearly. What I do on the job is a job. Out here, when we are off the clock, I'm your mother and you are my daughter."

"Mom, be happy. If this faceless man makes you feel like a teenager, go for it."

I teased, "He could be after your money and all. How would I know?"

Momma laughed out loud as she heard me say that. She knows I'm joking because that's just the way I am. She looked at me and spoke earnestly, "You are just like your dad, and you don't know how frightening that is. He took pride in his work, just like you. He wasn't as mean as you are to the potential suspects, but—"

I stopped her by asking, "Captain, what makes you think I'm mean?"

"Catherine, I know you and how you are. Not only that, your list of complaints is almost twenty miles long and could be longer, if I include the ones that were dropped."

"I get the job done, though," I spoke, prideful.

"You should be more mindful and easier. People do want our help. We don't want them afraid of calling us because they had some type of run in with you."

"Momma, being easy and mindful will get you shot in these streets, and I won't go down early or like that."

Politely, she touched my hand and spoke softly, "I know, baby."

"When will I meet this man?"

"Soon, I'm having a dinner here."

"Ok. What you cook today?"

"I cooked some yams, fried chicken, dinner rolls, and store-bought lemon cake."

"Let me get a plate."

"Bring my plate back."

"Ma, you know where I stay if I don't bring it back."

"I shouldn't have to come collect my things."

"If I don't bring it back, I will put it in the truck and take it to the station."

Momma gave me her warmest smile as I went in the house. Walking into the house was like walking back in time almost. Her house was spotless and smelled of baby powder and flowers. Her dishes were in the same place they always were as I fixed my plate and put everything back up. I went outside and sat beside Momma. She looked up when I retorted, "Ma, I'm gonna eat here, so I can leave your plate when I finish."

"There is some Kool-Aid in the fridge, did you get some?"

"No. I'll go back when I finish eating."

"I was told by my superior that Morton will be having an opening in a few months; as of right now, I want you there."

I almost got choked as I heard her tell me that. Puzzled, I stammered, "What?"

"You love dogs."

"Not dogs, just Beast. I love Beast."

"Well, Beast is a dog, like other dogs that will help us with the war on uncontrollable people and drugs."

"But Morton is the city PD. You know I like the county."

"If it clearly opens, I want you on it."

"Is this because you think I'm still a hazard to the department? If that is the case, I will change."

"No. It is because that is where you belong. You love the action that being on a drug task force can bring."

"We get plenty of action in the county."

"Not the type of action you need to express your typical behavior. You need to be in a position that you can handle the suspects your way. On the county PD, you can't do that. A lot of our calls are domestic violence, a tip on a suspect, shooting, and so forth. We even have some where people are helping to hide potential defendants."

"What if I won't take it?"

"If the job comes open and you won't take it, then I will put you on desk duty for weeks at a time until you do."

"Momma, you can't do that."

"I'm the chief. I can and I will."

"Why?"

She faced me with honesty in her face. From her look, I can tell she's been thinking about it for a while. She said, "I know you love the streets, and you love the excitement. We have it in Scott County, but you need more. Your ruthless behavior should be expressed more and by that being a part of a drug team will do that for you. If you are on SWAT, you kick in more doors and make more arrests, do stings and your talent will be more useful."

Looking afar off from her, I questioned, "Why the sudden change of heart?"

"I've been thinking about this for a while. I know I cannot contain your persona. I will help you find your way. Put that degree to work."

I ate a little more, because she'd almost spoiled my appetite. I questioned her nicely, "What if I don't like it?"

"If you really don't like it and the excitement isn't what you really want, then I will arrange for your return if I'm still in office."

"What you mean, if you still in office?"

"I plan on retiring very soon with a recommendation in mind."

"You don't think I'm good enough?"

"Your specialty isn't governing people; it's doing what you do best on the streets."

I was quiet for a moment before saying softly, "Give me some processing time and I will get back with you."

"Ok."

"Let me get up from here."

"What's the rush, Catherine?"

"You shipping me off and I don't like it, Ma."

"You will understand why later."

"I'm not patient, so I need to know right now."

"I'm being your mother and trust me on this, if you don't trust me on anything else."

Seeing her sincerity, I replied, "I trust you, Ma. I always have and why stop now?"

"Good, now give me a hug and you go home and get some rest."

"Ma, I'm not 10-8 until tomorrow night."

She laughed as she said, "I almost forgot you back on night shift. I was enjoying seeing you on days. I really did forget."

"Right. Don't ever put me on day shift again."

Momma laughed as she said, "Come in early tomorrow. You will be showing Investigator Cooley around the county."

"He is a big boy. Let Bell or Jackson do it."

"No, it's you, because that way I know you are not in any trouble."

"Ma, you know trouble finds me."

"Not while you are in his care, it won't."

"Fine what time?"

"Come in by four, but earlier if you can."

"Ok. You want me to take this plate back in and wash it?"

"You go on home, I'll do it."

I gave my mom a kiss on the cheek and left with Beast on the back of my truck. I arrived at home and Texan was blowing my phone up. I didn't respond and I won't respond until I get ready to; it won't be today. Beast jumped off the truck. I got out and fed him his dog food. He was eating like he was starving. I smiled because he is a healthy dog. I rinsed his tray off, went in the house and I locked the door.

It's almost four and Jarissa is stopping by for a few. I showered and picked up the Bible. *What a choice in reading,* I thought. I was amazed about the signs of the end times and how we as people look at the sky for what we think. So much stuff was being revealed, and my understanding became easy. I became so engrossed that I didn't hear the car horn blow.

I got up and peeped out the window. It was Jarissa and she knows not to get out the car if Beast is patrolling my yard. I stepped out the door and screamed, "Stand down."

Beast obeyed and I stood in the door and waved for Jarissa to get out the car. She got out and came in. We hugged. She sat down and I offered her something to drink, but she refused. However, she did ask, "What's up?"

Making sure I'm not out of line, I replied, "Jackson wants me to talk to you about your habit."

She gave me the "shut the hell up" look, although she didn't physically speak it. Jarissa retorted, "It's none of his business what I do."

"True, but he saw you in the car doing you in public."

She was quiet for a minute. I opened the conversation to say, "Speak what's on your mind. This is me you talking to. I'm here for you and I will give you my opinion if you ask for it, or if you don't. I love you and I'm here for you if you want my help, but I can't and won't force it on you."

"I understand, but I'm grown, and my habit doesn't interfere with my work."

"He said it doesn't interfere with your work, but you have a habit that will eventually cost you more than you could lose. We must uphold the law and that goes for one of our own. He only wants the best for you."

"You my girl and I love you, but let me do me," Jarissa stated as always.

"Alright, do you. I love you regardless even if you stay on the white girl, those jerkers or whatever you call them. What you do is your business, but when you do it in places other than home, it becomes a crime, and that crime makes it our business. Just be careful and work it out."

"You right."

Jarissa was getting nervous, and I could tell she didn't like the conversation. I knew she wouldn't, because no grown person wants another grown person to tell them what to do. I came in love and it's on her if she doesn't receive it. She stood up and verbalized, "I have to go."

I walked her towards the door and said, "I do appreciate you watching out for me and I will be more careful in the future."

"Ok."

Jarissa got in the car and drove off. I locked the door back, set the alarm and went to bed. The next morning, I woke up late and ate breakfast. I didn't sleep well at all. I tossed and turned, but I was thankful I did get some type of rest. I called Renee and her husband said she will be at work. I fed Beast and went back inside. My cell rang and I didn't look at the caller ID as I spoke, "Hello."

"I hear you babysitting this evening and can't get in the streets where the real work is at."

"Yeah, I plan to let you go unwatched, but I'll be back later."

We laughed as I asked, "Why you calling? You should be sleep."

"I'm always up early, you know that."

"No reason. I'm waiting on Jackson so we can get police gear in Pearl."

"Ok. Why didn't y'all ask me? I wasn't doing anything. I might need some new police gear."

"We figured you couldn't go because you taking big baby around the county and show him all the hot spots."

"Ha-ha, funny."

"Well, you do. Spend your morning that way because we have grown folk's things going on."

"If you don't mind, pick me up a black police toboggan."

"Where your money?"

"Are you for real right now?"

He laughed as he said, "I'll ask Jackson if he can spot you. I can't do it; you might forget and think you already paid."

"Bye, Bell."

Having this job requires a physically fit body, if only I could tell my wide hips that; I laughed as I got ready for my morning jog. Stepping outside, Beast was alert. I gave him his morning breakfast as I did my stretching to loosen my muscles. When I finished, so was Beast. With his roller collar in my hand, we got on the left side of the road. Beast always gets on the outside of me to face traffic.

CHAPTER 7

About half a mile towards Highway 35, I heard tires skidding my way. In a flash, I jumped out the way and a car almost hit Beast. Instantly, I knew it was Texan's ole girl because of the car. I waved my hands for them to stop, but they kept going. Rushing over to Beast, I spoke softly as I rubbed his head, "Boy, you ok, huh? We'll get 'em," I spoke with anger.

I started to turn around but decided against it. We headed on towards the store. We arrived there and took a break. The manager of the store asked me if I wanted a Gatorade. I accepted it with gladness. That is one of the things I love about being a "pig," you get some things half-off, if not free, because we are here to protect and serve the public.

Finishing my drink, I stretched a few seconds and started back towards home. My best friend and I didn't get halfway home when I saw the car on the side the road with a flat. They saw me coming and tried to play hard. Beast began barking and going into a heavy trot. I could barely contain his spirit as he headed straight towards the ones that tried running us over. "Stand down!" I screamed.

The occupants in the vehicle took off, but it was too late. Beast was all on the passenger. He had her up against the car, growling at her. Still with his roller collar in my hand, I took my time and walked up on her. I noticed Texan's ole girl was the one in the car. I put my face on the window and asked her, "Why you in the car? Get out and talk now! You almost hit Beast! I don't get down like that!"

"Get this dog off me!"

For my advantage, I asked in a sneaky way, "Tell that friend of yours to get out the car and I will get the dog off you."

Terrified, she screamed, "Get out the car! Get your ass out my car, so she will get this dog off me!"

The girl continued sitting there with her head pointed straight. I played them against one another. "I thought y'all were friends, but how is that if she isn't getting out the car? Looks like she's saving her own skin and not yours. What kind of friend do you have?"

"Get yo ass out my car!" the girl screamed again over her shoulder. Then, I saw a truck coming from a distance. "Stand down!"

Beast got down. The girl was frightened as the truck approached. I knew it was Captain. She stopped and looked before speaking, "Is everything alright, ladies?"

"Captain, all is well here."

Beast barked. Momma looked at the girl and must have seen a frightened look as she asked the girl more directly, "Is everything alright with you, young lady?"

The frightened girl said, "Tell her to get out my car!"

Captain looked at the driver and knew who it was. "What's going on here?"

The girl began rambling, "I was driving, and we saw her and her dog. My girl said, 'Let's make 'em run,' because they got into it a while back. I thought it was funny, so I made my tires screech as I took off towards them. When they got out the way, I went past them. We turned back around and that is when I had a flat. Her dog came at me and I'm afraid. She told me to tell my friend to get out the car and she will get the dog off me, and that is when you came, and she told the dog to stand down."

"You thought running someone over was funny?" Captain asked with a hint of tension.

"I did, but I wasn't going to hurt them, I swear."

"What about the lady in the car? What, she thought it was funny?"

"It was her idea."

"Let me make sure I got this right. You were driving this vehicle. Your friend makes a suggestion, about making an officer and her dog jump in a ditch. You both thought it was funny. You obliged and left the scene. You doubled back and had a flat. It is here, where this officer approached you with her dog. Is this all, correct?"

"Yes."

Captain got out her vehicle and stated, "Put your hands behind your back."

"What the hell for?"

"For using your vehicle as a weapon to do bodily harm to an officer and her police-acting dog. That is two counts. Sounds like a felony to me, Officer Le Beau."

"Wait," the girl said.

"Yes, please be quiet, because you have the right to remain silent. Anything you say can and will be used against you in a court of law. You have a right to an attorney. If you can't afford one, one will be appointed to you."

The girl turned around. She picked up the tire iron and aimed it at her window. I apprehended her as Captain got the driver out and read her, her rights too. Beast was on guard and barking, because this type of action gets him hype. Captain threw me a pair of handcuffs and I placed them on her. She got off the ground, yelling at Texan's ole girl. Captain called for a J-2 and a tow. About seven minutes later, blue lights were everywhere. The day shift cops, Officers Lopez and Uri came and took the two women to jail.

Momma gave me a hug and said, "This is the reason why I really wish you weren't on the streets, but I know you love them so."

"Momma, I was minding my own business, and they came at us."

"I know, but it doesn't stop me from worrying about you. Catherine, you are my daughter."

"Ma, I'm twenty-five."

"Catherine, I'm sixty-two."

"What has gotten into you lately? You have changed; you are so sentimental. Are you missing Daddy or something?"

"No, but I will always love your father. As for being sentimental, I do have a new man."

"I know, but you act like I can't take care of me and mine."

"Catherine, I was gonna wait, but I'm getting married."

"What the hell!"

Cars came through as we waited for the tow to come. I'm blown completely away. Ma questioned me softly, "You, ok? Catherine, are you ok?"

"Ma, I'm fine about it, just shocked and I never met him. How do I know he loves you?"

"He does and I love him too."

"Why can't you wait? I know y'all ain't been dating that long, for love to make you both want to get married in a rush."

"We are old and we don't have a lot of time left. We fit and we are happy. I just want you happy."

"I'm happy because you deserve it. I'm just shocked."

"What you about to do?"

"Go home and get ready for work."

"I'm not coming in today. I'm going back home and rest. You want me to take you both on to the house?"

"No, we will finish our daily run."

"Ok."

She turned around in the nearby driveway. She waved at me and drove off in the direction she came. *She must have forgotten why she was headed towards the store;* I thought as Beast, and I started back on our way home. Once we made it home, I gave Beast some water outside and I went in. Turning off the alarm, the semi-cool house felt nice. I sat in the chair and took a deep breath. My mind began to wander all over the place. Dumbfounded isn't the expression to describe how I feel right now.

I chuckled at that. Getting up, I showered and got ready for work. After listening to Momma, I put Texan and all my other sugar daddies on the block list. Turning the alarm on, I gave Beast his dinner and locked the gate behind me as I drove off towards McDonald's. This eating establishment was not happening; that line was wrapped around the building and packed. I went to Little Caesar's and ordered their Pepperoni Cheesy Bread instead.

It was about three and my girls were still at work. I don't need my music today, because I will be spending almost all my shift with Investigator Cooley, riding around. Pulling into the back of the building, I sat there and thought about him. *I wonder what his story is.* Bell and Jackson pulled up and I asked, "I thought y'all were in Pearl?"

"We were, but we heard about a 10-47 in Hillsboro."

"What was the disturbance in Hillsboro?" I asked.

They laughed at me. I asked again, "What 10-47 disturbance did you hear about?"

"You; our Scott County dynamite."

"If these hoes keep it up, this dynamite will blow a fuse and destroy all in its way."

We all got out and clocked in together. I went to the middle of the building and saw Jarissa. My best friend was finishing up her rounds. She saw me and yelled out, "What is happening on the county side of the building?"

I wasn't too surprised because she hears everything and nothing happens in this place that she doesn't know about. The

94

same goes for the County we all know what is going on. I replied, "Nothing. I came by to holler at you for a minute, but when you finish up, go to the dispatcher's office where Renee's at."

"Oh-oh, what's wrong?"

"What makes you think that?"

"You wanting us both there so you won't have to repeat it."

"Right. Hurry up, this can't wait, and I can't wait."

I saw the young cop and he gave me the middle finger. I yelled out in front of everyone, "Rookie, you have a 10-22."

"Who wants to see me here at the station and I'm already here?" he stammered.

Holding up my hand I began to open and close my fist while yelling, "My hand cracking your nuts."

All that were in earshot fell out laughing. He gave me a disgusted look and left out the area. My girl smirked and told me, "You shouldn't do him like that."

"He should have kept his mouth shut about how I do me."

"Cat, they say someone in the building is a snitch."

I looked around and responded softly, "Whatever is going on, be careful. We never know who is who around here, because people will do anything to get ahead."

"You right and I will, Cat."

We hugged as I went back to my side of the building. I sat in my area when Jackson and Bell sped out. I never knew snitching was going on because I'm too busy kicking in doors and making arrests. Since she is on the inside, I know she's going to figure it out. Their day started early by going on a 10-92 on Robert Butler Road. I remembered going on that call before to a brick house. I bet the lady there isn't on her medicine and that is why the 10-92 call came in. Looking up, I saw Investigator Cooley at the door. I checked my cell phone and saw he was early.

"You early?" I asked playfully.

"Hello, ma'am."

"A gentleman."

"I try."

"My name is Officer Cat Le Beau. Everyone around here calls me Cat, but the pranksters of the department call me Hell Cat."

"I know who you are," he stated with authority.

"Then you know how we do things around here."

"I don't care how y'all do things around here. I care about how I do things around here."

"You sound so confident, if not cocky. Tell me, is it true what they say about tall men?"

He walked up on me. "Only if it's true what they say about short women."

"It does have a sense of humor. It does have a sense of humor," I mocked.

Investigator Cooley stared down at me. I glared up into the friendliest set of extremely brown eyes I have ever seen. He gave me a warm smile and murmured, "Since our hellos are out the way, show me this great county."

For the first time in a long time, I stammered with words. *What's going on*? I thought as I spoke, "Let me run back and leave a message."

"Ok, that will give me time to put my things in my office."

Rushing off to see Renee, I caught her coming out of the bathroom. I remembered she told me she was sick on Saturday at the party. I had to check on her. Soon as I saw her, I asked in a hurry, "You feeling better?"

"I am thanks, but what's really wrong? You walking so fast."

"My shift just started, but I had told Jarissa to meet me up here."

"For what?"

"I will tell ya later. Investigator Cooley is here and he's 10-8."

"Ok, he is early, but what you want me to tell her?"

"Just tell her since he's ready for duty, I will get back at you both later, because when I get off, y'all will be coming on as 10-8."

"You right, we will be coming in as you get off. I guess that'll work."

I left Renee and asked Investigator Cooley, "You ready?"

"Yeah, let's go."

I walked in front of him, and he asked, "Which vehicle we riding in?"

"We can go in my patrol car."

"Here, let me get that for you."

He opened the door for me. I sat in the seat, mesmerized, with a silly girl look on my face. He got in and asked, "Are we leaving or what?"

"Yeah, I was lost for a minute."

"You never had a man open the door for you before?"

"No and that was so weird."

"I believe in treating a woman like a woman and no different, even if she puts herself in a man's place."

Leaving out, I asked, "What's a man's place?"

"Wanting to hit on you as you try to restrain her."

"Oh."

"Where are we off to first?"

"We are going to the top far end of the county first."

"What's the top far end?'

"Brusha."

I almost turned on some tunes, but I asked, "I hear you're Christian, is that true?"

He never looked at me as he responded, "I hear you're not, is that true?"

"You have a smart mouth."

"So, do you."

"Look. We may have started out on the wrong foot, but we will be working together. Our office space is side by side, and we will be seeing each other and working with each other, so whatever your problem is you need to push it out your butt and be done with it. We both have jobs to do, and we must do them to the best of our ability."

He didn't respond. He kept his cool as we rode down Highway 21, past Ephesus Road. I didn't say much and neither did he. I turned right onto Ringo Road when he said, "I'm sorry; I was not nice. I have a lot on my mind."

"You good."

"Where you say we are headed to?"

"It's a community called Brusha and there's one called H-town."

"Brusha, H-town?"

"To be honest, there are a lot of weird town names, and you must become familiar with them, because we have a lot going on back here and you need to know these areas."

"It'll take me some time, but I will know it like the back of my hand."

While we were out, various calls came across the air waves, but it was nothing serious. I was kind of glad no one went to jail, because I was not in the mood for paperwork or to restrain anyone for stepping out of line. Captain radioed us, asking how things were going and the Scott County Boys talked mad crap, which is always funny. I could tell he was getting the hang of how we act to each other, because he asked, "I can tell you all have a chemistry that allows you to joke and laugh as you do. That is a good thing when you are in a profession like this."

"If you don't enjoy the people you work with, you won't work here long. It's like you said, we have a chemistry, which makes working here worth the while. We all get along and we all are like family. I don't have any brothers, and these guys are the closet I have to having any. They make me laugh and I can talk to them about anything."

"Sounds like you love them."

"I do. They each have their own way of showing love, and they each have their own way of getting on my nerves but overall, I would not trade them for the world. I'm glad they are in my life."

He was taking in the scenery and observing as he inquired, "What do you do to get yourself started before you hit the streets?"

I glanced over and smiled. He must've thought I didn't hear him. Kindly, he asked, "Well, how do you get yourself ready for work here on the streets?"

"I listen to some hype music like Boosie, Gotti or Jeezy. That sets the tone for me."

"Oh. I think I have heard of them before."

"Really?" I said in full astonishment.

"Not really. I just wanted to see what you would say."

We laughed at that, and his laugh was pleasant, as well as a turn-on for me. It was enlightening. He asked another question. "You listen to them tonight?"

"No. I knew a lame was riding."

He laughed again. "A lame, huh?"

"Yes, a lame, a new kid on these streets; a you."

"So, I'm lame?"

"Until I see otherwise; you are a lame."

Cooley smiled as I reversed it on him by saying, "Now, how do you start your day?"

"That is an easy question. I bind the devil up and ask the Lord for strength and guidance as I do my job. I ask the Lord for protection for everyone on the job name by name, because our job can turn serious just like that. I'll read the daily scripture and that is that."

I wasn't prepared for that; I thought as he looked at me. That answer threw me all the way off guard. I had to say, "Wow. I never heard anyone say that before."

"That's because I'm different and uniquely put together by God *himself.* If Jesus doesn't cover you, who do you think has your back?" I was flabbergasted and couldn't answer his question. He smiled and asked, "You stumped?"

"That I am. You threw me off."

"What did you think I was going to say?"

"I don't know, but that wasn't it at all."

CHAPTER 8

We talked a little more about basic things pertaining to the job. I even let him drive. Time was moving as he listened to calls come across the radio. Deciding to go out on a call with Jackson and Bell, we showed up. I wanted to see how he acts in the field unscripted. They already had the situation under control, but I wanted to see for myself. So, did the guys. They let him talk to the person as we talked about him. I told them he's cool, and I think he will adjust working with us fine.

They all agreed. When the call was over, we drove for a while, and I was pointing out all the little areas we go to on this side of town. He was listening to me talk and he was talking back. I discovered he was in fact pleasant and interesting. I was honestly enjoying myself. His company was laid back and we laughed. Every now and then, we pulled into the store for a bathroom break or to get a bite to eat, but all in all what I heard about him wasn't like I thought. I had no idea time had gotten away from us.

Next thing we know, we had ridden all over the county and it was almost five am. We pulled back up to the station and I parked the patrol car. I got out and he said, "Officer Le Beau—"

"Call me Cat or Officer Cat."

He smiled and stated, "Cat, I really had a wonderful time with you showing me the county. I must admit, it is different, and I liked it very much."

"We saw the majority and if we must, we can do the same thing tonight; then it's back on the streets for me and whatever for you."

Investigator Cooley smiled and said, "Just call me Cooley."

"Ok, Cooley. I had a great time, and I will see you tonight."

He walked ahead and opened the door for me as we entered the building. Renee was taking a call and we each went to our desks. Every so often, I would see him looking up at me and smiling. I would only shake my head. When Captain came in, he stood up and then sat down. She and I looked at each other. He was doing stuff my dad used to do, and I rarely saw men do that when a woman entered a room.

His way of acting made me look at him as a real man and not one I have heard about since my dad's passing. Cooley was in fact a rare kind of man. Ma used her work tone to say, "Cooley, in my office."

"Good morning, Captain," I stated.

Looking exhausted, Captain stated, "I didn't sleep at all. I couldn't get comfortable, but good morning, Catherine."

"Oh. I'll see you later. It's time for me to get off and I want to leave out before the other two gets here."

"Why is that?"

"They have jokes."

She shook her head, and I left. During the entire drive, I haven't really talked to my girl since the other day. I forgot to check back and tell them about Ma and I hadn't even texted her or nothing. I guess I have been busy more than ever lately, but she will get at me. I was supposed to get at them this morning before I left, but being with Cooley made me forget.

All night, he'd been throwing me off with his answers and his attitude towards things. He makes me stammer on words and no man has ever done that; not even Ve-Lo. There is something about this one that is worth finding out more about.

The thoughts of Cooley were all on me as I unlocked the gate. For his eyes invited me to the sincere way he did small things for me. I see now sleep was not happening soon. Parking my truck, I noticed Beast didn't bark; he was asleep. I put his breakfast before him anyway. Wearing a geeky smile, I went into the house, turned off the alarm, reset it and locked the door. I strip while going straight in the bathroom. I showered and once that was done, I put on a nightgown and went to bed.

I managed to sleep. Upon waking up, I saw I had slept all afternoon, and it was soon time for work. That thought made me smile like crazy. I bathed, got dressed and for the first time, I couldn't decide on what kind of perfume to wear. *What am I doing*? Here I am, can't make up my mind about how to smell. I'm a police officer and I'm acting like I have a regular gender job.

Finally, I sprayed on some PINK perfume and pulled my hair back into a ponytail. Placing on my vest and shirt, I admired the view in the mirror. Turning on the alarm, I locked the door and went to check on Beast. He was trotting around his area. I fixed him more water and went over to his small fridge and picked up a dripping blood red deer ham. Making sure it didn't waste on me, I put it in a pan. Beast was eating like a mad man; it was the blood.

I thought of a scripture about how the blood of Jesus cleanses us and it's in *his* blood we can get healed and nourished as we need. My eyebrows lifted as I applied scripture to just seeing Beast eat the dripping blood. Renee said if you read *his* word, it will open up to you in real life. She was right. Sighing a happy sound, I got in my truck and left. I got to work, and Bell was there. He asked, "How was your night showing Cooley around?"

"I enjoyed it and I must admit, I didn't want to do it, but I'm glad I did."

"Just checking." Bell said.

"Checking on what?" Cat asked.

Bell laughed and Jackson came in. It was unusual to see him in an over and beyond good mood. Today, he seemed like a new man. Bell asked, "You excited about work, give me some of that, man? I can sure use it."

"Man, I'm always excited about work," Jackson replied.

I added, "He's excited because we get to kick in some doors today and stop some lawbreakers."

"Where we going for a 10-6?" Jackson asked.

"To the Party House in Steele." Cat spoke.

"We always go there," Bell commented.

"We have to go where the ABC men want to go, and they got a tip for illegal liquor being sold there." Jackson remarked.

"They need to leave the mom-and-pop places alone and go after some real places," I added.

Cooley walked in, saying, "If they are breaking the law, they are breaking the law. We go after them all. No small stone should be unturned." We all stared at him and started back talking as if he didn't say a word. Cooley got settled and asked, "Are we going on the raid?"

"You may not, but I am. It's been a while since I kicked a door in with ABC and I'm not going to miss that," I answered.

"Yes, you are," a voice chimed in.

We all turned around in haste and saw it was Captain. I knew she meant what she said. I began to almost beg by saying, "What? Come on, Captain. It's the ABC."

"You already have a job and that is to show Investigator Cooley around the county."

My eyes pleaded with her. "I have showed him around."

"Show him again," she commanded.

Captain stood there and I replied, "Yes ma'am."

Almost immediately when her door closed, Jackson said, "Guess we have to get another stick of dynamite from somewhere, because this one is a dud."

"Funny. Y'all wait. I'm going to go and talk to her," I told them.

"You better make it quick, because soon as they show up, we riding out." Bell stated.

I took off to her office. Knocking on the door, she said, "Come in, Catherine."

I walked in and closed the door silently. She said, "You need to show him around."

"I did that yesterday." Cat replied.

"That was yesterday. I need you to take him around the communities today. Not drive by them, but take your time and show him the areas, so he can be familiar with them."

"Why is this so important to you?"

"If I retire, the position will be offered to Cooley."

With a surprised tone, I questioned, "You really plan to leave the force?"

This time she sat back in her seat to reply. "I told you that day when you came over and ate at the house."

"I remember. I just thought it was just a thought you were having."

"You know this job can be something serious and I'm getting old."

"You right, but you already old," I spoke as she laughed.

"Worrying about you and your list of complaints and making sure we handle the crime is getting heavy for a woman like me, but I will do my job very well while I have it."

"You have to do what is best for you, but you shouldn't push me to do what I don't want to do. This has become my life, and I love what I do."

"Catherine, please be cool while I'm here."

"Anything else?" I asked in a smart way.

"Yeah, you will be getting a new partner and a new position."

"What are you talking about now, Captain?"

"You will be doing training for new hires and if anything concerns the K-9 Unit, you will do those as well."

"Huh?"

"It's not my doing. It's coming from the top and because of your educational background; you must move up the chain. Think of the money you will be making and how much safer you will be."

"I don't care for money. I like doing what I do, but you are confusing me."

"How?"

"One day you tell me in a few months if the position comes open, you want me to transfer out to Morton on the K-9 Unit, and now you tell me I'll be doing trainings. Which is it, Captain?"

"As of right now, you are to train with Cooley because things are changing, and it was told to me that every department will have two investigators."

I only sat there and stared at her. She didn't say another word. I got up and she said, "Don't breathe a word to anyone. The time isn't right yet."

No words came out of my mouth as I closed the door. Cooley was standing there as he asked, "You, ok?"

Flatly, I said, "You ready to ride?"

"Yeah."

Bell and Jackson were gone with the ABC, and I hate I missed out on that, but I can't do anything about it. Cooley and I went to the back, and he opened the door for me. I didn't care who was around I only wanted to get out the building. So much was happening, and I needed to process the information my mother just gave me. Cooley stated, "Hate you missed your door-kicking experience."

I still didn't say a word as I decided to take him through Morton and work my way from there. What he said next captivated me. "I'm here if you want to talk."

"I already have a best friend named Jarissa and a best dog named Beast. I don't need to talk to you."

He was quiet and then he said, "Yeah, I know Jarissa quite well, but you are thinking that me being here has changed your life."

"It has!" I yelled.

"You are yelling, now we are getting somewhere."

111

I made it to Morton and took a right on Highway 13. After crossing the tracks, I stated, "You are so right. Ever since you came to this department, it has been crazy for me. I can't kick in doors and go on 10-6's because I have to babysit you."

Cooley snickered a little when I said that. He replied out loud, "That's not true. You were a short fuse long before I came onto the scene. If I'm not in error, you already knew about the possibility of transferring or whatever before I started. Catherine, learn how to channel your anger and keep it real with yourself."

Pulling the car over I faced him to say, "Let us get this straight. My mother doesn't want me to be an officer because it's too risky. She wants me to have a decent job, get married and have children. That is how she wants me to live."

"And what's wrong with a parent watching over their child?"

"That's not what I want."

"What do you want? What do you really want, Cat?"

"I want to be left the hell alone to do what I want."

"When you accomplish being left alone to do what you want, then what?"

I turned the ignition back on and pulled back onto the highway without saying another word to him, because I was on the verge of going off on him. No one has ever challenged me to think about my answers. It had never crossed my mind before—what all I wanted to do or how I wanted to get the things I need done. Now, what I really want to do with my life is weighing heavily on my mind.

Silently as ever, along with the politeness and sincere words, Cooley spoke "You must look at it from her point of view. You are her only child, and she cares about you and things connected to you. She knows you are grown, but being a parent never stops because the child grows up; it continues. There is nothing wrong with her wanting the best for you."

Bluntly and boldly, I proclaimed, "Forget her watch, I can watch me."

"You can't possibly fully understand the entire concept, because you are not a parent. You don't know how it is to be a single parent, and to do your best to take care of your child alone. You see, I can sympathize with your mom, because I'm doing just that. I know my son is going to grow up and I'm with that. I'm not with him disrespecting me as if I'm yesterday's news. I will respect his opinion about how he wants to live his life, but he will not disrespect me about doing my job as his parent."

We were quiet before he inquired, "Have you ever been in love?" I snapped my head towards him. "Let me say it differently, can you be loved?"

"Can you?" I retorted with no sympathy.

"I can be loved, and I was once loved by the love of my life. In short, we all crave to be wanted and needed. We are human, after all."

He was quiet as I asked with more compassion, "What happened to your wife, if you don't mind telling me?"

Cooley tilted his head towards me. "Her name was Para, and she grew up being the only child of a hard-working mother. Quite naturally, we wanted to have a house full of children. But, while she was pregnant with Preston, she lost a lot of blood and needed a blood transfusion. I had just told her that I was so proud of her, and I loved her. She gave me a pleased and loving look. I stepped out the room to go tell her parents our son was born and when I went back to see her, they told me she was in ICU because she slipped into a coma and never regained consciousness."

That shocked me. Now, I know why no one ever spoke about his wife because they never knew the story. I looked at him and said with empathy, "I'm so sorry. I really am."

"Thank you. I know I am changed and that is fine. It's not that I don't have a sense of humor, because I do. I guess I transformed when the responsibility of being a single parent fell on me. I have to be a role model to my son and do what is right, even if he is so young. I must follow God before I can teach my son how to be a man of God. I don't want to raise him up worldly and if I don't live right or do my best to live right, he will grow up living worldly. My job is to lead by example and being that I'm a man, I must do just that. So yes, it may look crazy that I open doors for women or treat them with respect, but that is who I am and how I want my son to be. I haven't done a lot of respectful because I'm more of a watcher than the center of attention."

"You need someone in your life to help you loosen up."

"I haven't found anyone that made me want to do that, yet."

We rode in silence for the entire stretch of Highway 13. When we came to the funny curve, I stated, "This is Contrell-Lena, well some of it. I'm going to turn off here on Hillsboro-Ludlow Road on the right."

He wrote a few notes down as I turned onto the road. I was thinking about all he has told me and decided to let him know. "After hearing what you did, I have a new respect for you."

"You do?"

"Yeah. I thought you were a stick-in-the-mud kind of guy that didn't want to have fun, or didn't care to be around co-workers; at least that is what the word is around the PD."

Cooley gave me a smile and we made it to Hillsboro. I turned to him to say, "I know you know where we are."

"I do."

I crossed Highway 35. I drove by Scott Central School and went a little further to turn down Gum Springs Road. When I began to go down the small road, he questioned, "Where are we going?"

"This is a cut off to Steele-Town, not far from Bell's crib."

"Oh, ok."

"What's the deal about you and my best friend anyway?" I wanted to know.

"Only friends."

"Only friends?" I waited to see if he would say more.

"I met her back here and we talked on the phone about various things and that was it. We didn't keep in touch."

"So, you not interested in her?"

"No, I may have someone else in mind."

The way he said that made me feel funny all over. It was like a smooth texture that feels just right, and I don't want it to stop. I cut my eye towards him and he was looking out the window. I hated we arrived at the end of the dirt road. I took a left on Old Jackson and headed towards King Road. I saw a pedestrian, so I rolled down the window and stopped. He saw me and raised his hands to say, "I haven't broken the law today, Officer Hell Cat."

"You good for now. What the business is?"

He laughed when he spoke. "Nothing's moving. Everybody's laying low maybe, I guess they know either you in the hood or the feds in town."

"Is that right?"

"Hell yeah. We all know you don't play. You one of the one's we wish would quit or transfer out into another field. Shit, we can't make a hustle with you showing up out the blue."

Cooley laughed. I looked over at him to say, "What you laughing at?"

He shrugged his shoulders and Stuck Up asked, "Who ya got wit ya?"

"This is Investigator Cooley."

"How you doing, Cooley?" Stuck Up said as he extended his hand for Cooley.

Cooley reached around me and spoke, "I'm good, how about you?" as he shook his hand.

"Man, I'm good, knowing she's in the car and not on my ass. Keep her in there."

We laughed, but I said, "Hate to break up the friendly meeting but we have to see more."

"Take it easy, man," Stuck Up said as he backed up away from the patrol car.

I drove off and Cooley was still smiling. I asked, "What?"

"You have them afraid of you or something?"

"No. When you a woman in a man's world, you have to have a hard-on and an attitude to match. I'm short, so I must have the whole package or be eaten alive."

"I see, Officer Wild Cat."

I continued driving as I asked, "What made you want to be an investigator anyway and not just that, but come to our county?"

"You don't waste time, do you?"

"Why should I? You either going to answer it or you ain't. I thought we were having a moment."

"I used to be on SWAT, but when my wife began to have complications, I transferred out and put my education to use. I have a PhD in Criminal Justice and a master's in criminal law. When she passed away, I continued to stay in Florida. When this position came open, I decided that new scenery would be good for my son and me. I thought, why continue to live in Florida? The more I thought about it, the more it made sense. My wife is gone and there's nothing holding me back. I wanted to leave anyway and taking it became a priority."

"What you think so far?"

He looked over at me. "Let's just say I'm warming up to it."

I went right on King Road and passed Steele Light House Church and drove slower. Luckily, I was on my side of the road because a car jumped the hill and scared me. He and I both hollered. Making a U-turn, I hit my siren and thrust on my lights. His tone became assertive. "What you doing?"

"Were you not in the same car? You didn't see the car almost hit us?"

I took off behind the car as fast as I could. The car turned on Old Jackson and didn't stop. Cooley got on the loudspeaker and commanded the driver to pull over. They didn't. At this point, I'm going eighty miles per hour. The car slowed down and came to a stop at the section of Old Jackson and Highway 21. In haste, I opened my door and drew my gun. Cooley did the same as he commanded the suspects to get out with their hands up.

The passenger got out first. Cooley commanded him to walk back towards the sound of his voice. The youngster did. Next, he commanded the driver to get out and do the same. To my surprise, it was a girl. Cooley and I left the doors and went to the suspects. He handcuffed the boy, and I got the girl. Trust

119

me I wasn't nice and with her on her stomach, I placed my knee in her back with a lot of pressure.

"You have your knee in my back," she screamed out.

"You almost hit me so my knee in your back is the least of your worries."

I pulled the small girl to her feet, and she appeared to be no more than fifteen and the boy was about the same; except he was thicker. He and I walked the juveniles back to the front of the patrol car. Cooley began to ask them their names and they wouldn't tell. I stated, "This isn't some damn show you see on TV. The officer asked you, your names. You need to tell him."

The two didn't say a word. I asked, "Are there any drugs, weapons or contrabands in the vehicle we don't know about but should?" They still didn't say a word. I asked again, "I guess answering our questions and telling us why you were driving so reckless is out?"

The girl said, "We don't have to tell you anything, pig, because we plead the fifth."

"Yeah, that's right, what she said about the fifth," the immature boy agreed.

"Y'all don't even know what the fifth is, but ok. Officer Cooley, read them their rights while I call a tow."

"You can't take us to jail. We are under fifteen. We will only go to a holding cell for kids," the boy stated.

"We will see about that, kids. We could have called your parents, but you want to be hard, so I treat you hard."

I called for a tow. When we placed them in the back of the car, we put on gloves and searched the car. We found some marijuana seeds, a case of beer, which, the county part of Scott County is dry and that was it. These two children endangered our lives for nothing but misdemeanors. Cooley smiled at me and said, "You enjoy doing this for a living, don't you?"

Stopping what I was doing to look at him and almost acting shy, I stated, "It is out here I can make a difference, talk smack and almost throw my weight around. When you break the law, I don't have any nice feelings about you; especially when you endanger my life and the life of my co-worker. Usually scare tactics work but when they don't, I treat them like they are any regular suspect."

He laughed and started back searching. I spoke before I realized it. "You have a nice laugh."

"Thank you."

"You should do it more often."

He didn't respond, but he laughed. The tow truck came and we got back in the car. We took the minors to the station and had them in holding until their parents could be notified.

121

He and I got back in the car and got back on Highway 21. This time, I took him past Old Jackson Road to end up on Beulah Road.

"What's off in here? It looks like only a few houses exist."

"It's a few houses and we do drive in and out to make our presence known. For the most part, it is quiet and peaceful. We never have a problem over here."

"Oh."

CHAPTER 9

I showed him all the houses on Beulah Road and headed back out. Once I faced Highway 21, I decided to take him back down Highway 21. I took a left on Highway 21 and a left on Old Jackson Road. We passed the Union Grove Church, and we went further. We passed Mt. Hebron Church and the big pond. We took a right into Jamestown. He was surprised about the road being a circle. Cooley began speaking, "This seems like a nice quiet neighborhood."

"It is and can be, but like every other hood; you have your people that will break the law."

"This seems like a retirement place."

"There are older working people here. They watch out for each other and will call the law on each other."

"Technically, it's a neighborhood crime watch from within."

"Yeah, and just a few weeks ago we got a tip on a local joker pimp, but when we started to set up a checkpoint, a different suspect showed up. We chased the suspect all the way to the fence row of that house in the back field. When we caught him, I was pissed."

"Why?" Cooley asked.

"He had no priors, no warrants; he had nothing."

"Why did he run?"

"He claims he thought we were after him and how he had heard about a lot of police brutality in the South."

"Where was he from?"

"Louisiana."

We laughed while I concluded, "Louisiana is still in the South, and they have their share of police crime like anywhere else. The difference is, we haven't killed anyone; have been wanting to but haven't this far."

"If the suspects would obey the law or if we give them a command, no harm will come to anyone, but you have those that make something out of nothing, Cat. When they do that, our lives are in danger, and I plan to go home to my son every night. So, if I have to empty fifteen rounds, I will empty them with reason. We officers are here to protect and serve and I know there are some crooked cops out there but for the most; we all love our jobs and place ourselves in harm's way all the time just to protect people who may want to harm us."

"I do agree."

As we left Jamestown, I took a left and then a sharp right. I spoke, "Now this is Oliver Drive."

"It seems nice."

"It is nice. Crime rate isn't too high here because of police visibility and most of these people go to work about the same time and they arrive about the same time. However, the traffic on this road is low. I must admit, they are much older people here that keep a watch while the others are gone and that helps."

"They are our very own neighborhood crime watchers?"

"Yes. Any vehicle that comes through here is suspect. Believe me, someone has written down everything about the car."

"That's good."

"It helps make our job easier."

We made it to the end of Oliver Drive, and I was about to take a right, until he began talking, "Let me guess. We are on our way to Sebastopol?"

I pulled over at the old Shaw's Grocery and stated, "No, Sebastopol is a small town that has their own police, although they are in Scott County."

"Oh. Ok."

I took a right on Highway 21 and turned left on Robert Butler Road. He asked, "What's back here?"

"This is one of the quietest neighborhoods in our area. There is second to none in crime. The people here are again older and traditional, sort of."

We rode all the way past old man Jones' Place and turned around. He asked, "Why we turn around for?"

"If we would've kept going, we would've been in Leake County and that is out of our district."

"Oh."

I began to drive further and decided to take a right. Cooley asked again, "Where does this lead to?"

"This is another community called Murrell-Town. It is also quiet and peaceful. They have church-going people on this street."

Cooley laughed as he made a joke, "They probably prayed the enemy out of their community."

"Possibly," I spoke with a smile.

We turned around and faced Robert Butler Road. This time I took a right and made it back to Highway 21 as I looked over at him and said, "Before I take you back towards town, let me take you to this community."

I went left on Highway 21 and took the next right. Cooley asked, "Is it also quiet?"

"It is a close-knitted community and it's like all other communities. You have this and that, but you never hear about it. They keep to themselves, and we don't have a problem with that at all."

"What do you call this area?"

"It's known as Hawkins Road, but the street calls it Over-In-The-Woods."

"That's different."

I smiled some. "It is and every community has its pros and cons."

I drove him to both loops and took a right to turn around. We came out and went back on Hawkins Road. We were facing Highway 21 again and this time, I took a left and then a right by Miracle Temple Church. The road was quiet and dark as he asked, "Where we going now?"

"This is another part of the area we patrol. We are going by the Curve first, then through Harperville.

"What you think of these communities so far?" He asked as I drove on.

"If they don't give me any problems, we won't have any trouble."

We came out facing Highway 35. I took a left and went down Highway 35 South. We were almost at the Northside Store. I asked, "You want to stop and get something to eat?"

"Uh, nah. It's been a long night, but I have enjoyed your company this far."

I passed through the intersection and kept straight. He didn't say a word as I drove, but I had to ask, "You must have thought I was going to be mean or something?"

127

"Nah, I didn't know what to expect, especially the way you grabbed ahold of the boy's balls with your hands."

We giggled. I had almost forgotten all about that, but I responded, "Oh that."

"Yes, that. It was too funny, and I laughed at that all night."

"I bet he will be careful the next time he crosses me or tries to put me on blast."

We stopped at the red lights and kept going. Soon, we arrived at the station, and we sat there. I didn't want to get out and neither did he. Cooley asked, "You want to talk some more?"

"I do, but it's almost time to clock out."

We both were quiet then he asked, "Cat, what you got planned for your next two days off?"

"Nothing, if I'm not hanging out with Jarissa and Renee."

"You want to go out, not a date, but to talk or something? We all need someone who isn't on the in-crowd, even if it's just to listen to our crazy ideas, or just to make us smile in some form."

"That will be nice and you right. Sometimes I want to scream and lately, I feel like doing just that."

"Every smiling face isn't a happy one."

"Here's my number, just text me the day."

He took my number and programmed it into his phone. I got out and he stayed in. Something is happening and I can't explain it. I'm no longer thinking about going home and seeing my friend. I'm thinking of him. I couldn't go to sleep when I got off. Since I've been patrolling with Cooley, I haven't been able to think of anything but him from his smile, his laughter, his tall body and everything about him. All I do is lie around and daydream about him; wanting to see him and smell his cologne. The way he laughs, the way he looks at me does something to me. I can just think about him and smile. My phone vibrated, interrupting my thoughts.

Thinking it was Cooley; I dashed to it. Seeing it was a text; I saw it was my girl telling me to let her and Renee in. I went to the front door and yelled, "Beast, stand down."

I'm so glad I have on a matching Superman set of pajamas and socks, because I was not going out, if Cooley didn't call. Seeing them walk up and my faithful companion in his post, I wished it was Cooley coming to see me instead. I stood in the door as they came in. The first thing my best friend asked is, "What is this I hear about you and Cooley?"

"Jarissa, before she answers that. Let her tell us why is she trying to make Superman look sexier by having a cut-off top?" Renee asked in a joking tone.

"I'm the new sexy for Superman," I said as I twirled around.

I smiled and Renee clapped her hands. Locking the door behind me, I spoke bluntly, "How about you girls sit down so we can talk, before you try and get all up in a woman's business?"

They both sat in their usual seats as I asked if they wanted something to drink. They both declined, because I know they're ready for me to tell them something. Renee asked first, "Tell us all about it."

Crossing my legs Indian style, sitting on my furniture, I stated, "There is nothing to tell really."

"Tell us what the really is."

I looked over at my girls to say, "He is cool people."

"That isn't what we heard?" Jarissa stated.

"What have you heard?" I questioned back.

"Nothing, but he wants to take you out," Jarissa said in a strange tone.

"It's not a date, if that is what you are thinking," I retorted.

"So, it is true. He is taking you out." Renee said.

"No. He basically asked if I would like to talk or even go to the park. I told him to contact me whenever and he said ok."

"Could it be love, Cat Le Beau?" Renee asked.

"No, it's nothing to do with love. Besides, you have to be in a relationship longer than me just knowing him a little while. I don't think he's, my type."

"Cat, that is the second time you have said that to me," Jarissa stated.

"And this is the second time I tell you the same thing," I replied.

"Tell me, does he like you or something? I'm dying to know all the things you won't tell," Renee asked with a hint of interest.

I answered, "I don't think it is like that, right now."

"What is it like, because he liked me like that to?" Jarissa spoke as she stood up.

Renee and I looked her way as I sparred back to her before standing up, "He told me he was like a pal to you. He also stated there wasn't anything going on so keep the bullshit moving like you doing your mouth."

Jarissa spoke out from nowhere as she kept her facial expression cold and heartless, "If you weren't my best friend; I would wipe the floor with your short ass."

"If you weren't my best friend, I would watch you try to wipe the floor with your high ass," I stated back to her because I'm not afraid.

131

She and I were squared off. Looking down on me, Jarissa spat, "You sound like you want him."

"Sounds like you have a problem with him not wanting you."

"I'm just saying," Jarissa snapped.

"Well, don't say," I said back to her.

"I can say what I want, and I think you want the wrong man."

"I can want anyone I choose to, like your baby daddy," I spoke to her.

"What?"

"Before ya met him, he used to come see me. I didn't give him the pussy. You did; with his broke ass," I told her.

"You a dirty, trick-ass, short bitch."

"Jarissa, what; I didn't tell you? It must not have been any of your motherfucking business who was trying to fuck me. But trust me; I told you; you just didn't listen."

Renee added as she was doing her best to squeeze between us, "She did tell you because I was there, and I was stunned that you still gave him play."

"Cat, if snakes are in the same damn family and they eat each other, what made me think we were any different?" Jarissa stated.

132

Renee made a comment that didn't faze me. "We family and family fight and we stick up for one another. Not only are we blood family, but we are a working family. Whatever is going on let it ride and pull together."

"Jarissa, if you want Cooley and you think you can have him; I'll back off. I'll let you have a go at him to see if you can do it."

"Naw, you work it," she told me.

"Then, what was the problem just then?" I asked.

"Nothing. It was nothing," she responded.

"It had to have been something for you to come in my house, and threaten to kick this ass over nothing," I explained.

"It was nothing," Jarissa replied.

"Well, J. Keep those nothings to yourself. I don't have time to try and figure your nothings out," Renee spoke.

We sat down and started laughing. We used to do that to Renee a lot, because she was the peacemaker whenever Jarissa and I would disagree with one another or with another girl. Somehow, the way we acted in front of Renee felt real. It almost felt like Jarissa is feeling envious of me and for what; I don't know. Sometimes when we play, I can tell it was all a joke but today to hear her and see how she was acting made me think it was more than just for play.

133

I really felt she was real, but I had to play it off because the time was not right. I have no idea what is on her mind, but she better come with it and tell me. I let it ride as I said, "So far we have only spent a few hours with each other and that has been it."

"Two or three hours are a few. You both have spent twenty-four hours and from what I hear, you will be his partner," Renee added in.

"How you hear that?"

"I told you on the inside you hear everything," Jarissa added.

"She's right, Cat. You hear everything on the inside," Jarissa added.

"Sisters, let me be frank about it. He is different than any man I met. At this very moment, he and I are co-workers. I'm showing him the communities and that is it. Do I like him? He's nice. Do I want to get in the bed with him? Not now, other stuff has to happen first."

"Other stuff like him tasting!" Jarissa exclaimed.

"That could be it."

Jarissa hooted and hollered at that line. I was beginning to wonder what the change of attitude was all about. I stated, "He is a gentleman, and I have to act like a lady."

"Only in a married bed should those things be done, you two," Renee mentioned to us.

I don't let just any man get my goods and almost all of them have to pay for it," I said with a smile.

Renee stated, "Cat, how about you tell us what you had to say before you dashed off with Investigator Cooley."

"Oh yeah. Brace yourselves."

I waited a few more minutes and said, "My momma, your captain, your aunt is getting married."

They both looked at me and laughed. I knew then there was something I was behind in knowing. Trying to figure out what they thought was funny; I asked honestly, "What's funny about that?"

"Girl, we knew because her attitude changed."

"Why didn't you tell me?"

"I wasn't for certain and besides we workdays with her, so we see her more than you do. We get a chance to pick up on many little things going on," Renee brought to my attention.

"We told you we hear everything on the days," Jarissa said as she sat back onto the couch.

Throwing a pillow, Renee stated, "I guess I have to tell you both my secret."

Jarissa and I stared at Renee because it isn't like her to gossip or tell any of her business. With keen ears, my best friend and I glared at her sister with eagerness. We placed ourselves on the edge of our seats to hear. We didn't want to miss a thing coming out of her mouth. At first, I couldn't make out what she was saying because she was literally screaming but when I finally heard the words, "I'm having a baby."

My best friend and I began to jump up and down as we rushed over to her. I couldn't believe it. Renee and her husband were high school sweethearts, and they are only twenty-seven. I like hearing good news about good people and these two are it. I was overjoyed at the news. My cousin concluded, "I'm expecting in five months."

"You plan to announce it at the party?" Jarissa asked her.

"No and what party?" Renee wondered.

"I think tomorrow evening and it's the party my mom's having to announce her engagement. Oh, you both didn't know?"

"I knew," Jarissa said.

"She might have mentioned it, but I been going through my own thing. I might have forgotten but why during the week?" Renee wanted to know.

"I think he does something on Saturdays and church on Sundays."

"Oh."

Renee asked, "If the dinner is tomorrow, then you must be going on the little thing with Cooley today?"

"He hasn't called or texted yet, so I don't know when it is. It supposed to have been on one of these days off, but nothing so far," I said.

"If you don't want him, I will take him," Jarissa spoke to make her petition known.

"He is a grown man and if you feeling him, tell me because I don't like beating my own cousin out over a man. I'm doing my best to give you a fair shot at him."

Renee laughed and Jarissa stated, "Go for it. It'll be nice to hear about you all over headquarters and place a bet on you both."

"You gone too far, right now we are just friends and I'm not trying to be a step-momma. You have to take me slow before things get any further for him and me."

"There's nothing wrong with being a stepmom. You get a chance to practice before you have yours."

"And mess up this figure? I beg to differ because it is a lot when you have to be a leader to a child."

I heard a horn blow, and we all stopped talking and we all went to the window to see who it was. My best friend squealed, "It's Cooley. He's getting out and pulling a roller cart with him."

"You got to be fucking kidding me!" I exclaimed as I dashed to the window to look for myself.

He's getting out and Beast wasn't trying to attack him. I was stunned to see my best dog in the world not protecting me. It looked like Beast and Cooley were on the same level, being bold and calm. I was stunned and didn't know what to do. Renee and Jarissa were just as surprised as I was. Cooley walked right up to the front door and rang the doorbell. I whispered, "Act normal."

I didn't ask who it was. I opened the door right up. He smiled and spoke, "Good evening. I usually don't pop up, but I'm trying to do things out the norm with you."

"You good," I stated with a smile as wide as a smile can get.

He must have seen Renee, and he asked in a surprised tone, "Did I catch you at a bad time? I mean, I can come back."

CHAPTER 10

Moving out the way, he gave me a smile back as I allowed him to enter. He spoke to my girls, and I said, "They were just leaving."

"We haven't been here long," Jarissa asked.

"I can come back later, Catherine, if that will be better for you?" Cooley said.

Jarissa mumbled with a smile, "Catherine? No one calls you that."

"No, you are here, and they were leaving as you blew the horn."

Renee got up and put her hands on her sister's hand as she said with a motion, "Come on, girl. We have other stuff to do, things to plan and I don't have all day."

"You always have to ruin the fun, Renee," Jarissa said in a teasing tone.

"Cat doesn't need us. We can catch up later."

I opened the door and walked them to their car. We gave each other a hug and said we loved each other. We have been best friends all our lives and no dick is coming between us; there are too many out there for us to have, then to fight over. Renee spoke with joy, "We want all the details."

"I know I can see it on your face."

"Don't leave anything out, Cat," Jarissa said.

When they left, I closed the back gate and put Beast back there. Entering the house with anticipation, I saw Cooley was still standing there. He smiled as he motioned for me to come on in as he made a statement, "Have a seat."

"Thank you."

"What brings you by here today?"

"I wanted to surprise you, and I guess I'm the one who got the surprise."

"You fine just forgive me for the way I'm dressed. I got up, showered and put this on, not expecting company from you or anyone."

"You look beautiful."

I blushed hard and replied, "Why thank you, Cooley."

"I know I said I wanted us to go to the park or something, but I thought about cooking you dinner here at your house."

My mouth gave an enormous smile; I could barely believe it. I asked him nicely and almost shyly, "Is that what you are pulling in the cart?"

"Yes, I want to do something for you that I don't believe anyone has done before."

I still couldn't stop the smiling as I replied, "You succeeded. No. no one has ever done that."

"I gather it's ok for me to do this?" he asked as if I was going to say no to a fine man cooking and catering to me.

"It is. You have just made my day like no other."

"How about spaghetti covered with meatballs simmered in marinara sauce, three-cheese garlic bread, side salad, Hershey's pie and sweet tea for the drink?"

"I like that. Do I need to change?"

Cooley stared at me. He replied as if I was the only thing that mattered when he said out loud, "No, you are lovely the way you are, and this is you in your natural environment. I don't need make up or a made-up woman to empress me. I want to say that you being you is why I'm clearly fascinated with you."

I tried to make light of the heavy moment by saying back to him, "You sure it's not because you need a companion and that is why you like me so well?"

"No. I can have any woman I want because that is what the devil will give me. I can even have sex on any given day; therefore, having a woman or any woman in my life isn't the issue. The enemy will do anything to get you off track and giving you want you think you need is Satan's number one goal. In truth, I'm unusual and I need an unusual kind of girl in my life."

The only thing to come out my mouth was, "What am I?"

"Right now, someone I'm taking things as they come. You also happen to pique my interest."

Liking what he just said, I implied sweetly, "Come this way. Let me show you, my kitchen."

We went a few feet into the kitchen. He was admiring my cabin home. I can't believe this is happening to me. This is so unexpected and never happened to me before, but here I am, and it is happening. I can't figure him out and it strikes my curiosity. Cooley interrupted my thoughts when he spoke. "I like your home. It has a feeling of peace to it."

"Thank you. It's a two-bedroom, two bathrooms, with medium kitchen, dining room and living room, which sits on two acres."

"This is a nice spot. It's family friendly."

Cooley was taking his things out of the bag, and I stated, "Here, let me help."

"No. I want you to rest and enjoy, for this is your day."

I went back to the living room and sat back on the recliner. Almost twenty minutes later, he came in and brought me a glass of red wine.

"Thank you. What happened to the tea?"

"You're welcome and I took a guess that red wine would've been better for someone like you."

"You right again."

He sat in the chair Renee always sits in. He sipped a little wine, then asked, "No one has ever done this for you before?"

I couldn't help but smile as I replied to him, "You are really the first man to be in my home. I normally don't invite men into my home because they are faceless, and I don't need to be reminded of them whenever I turn around in my home."

"I feel special."

"You must be, you in here catering to me and I'm allowing it."

I took a few more sips of wine and pointed out, "Something smells really nice," indicating the food he was cooking

"Wait until you taste it."

He got up and went back into the kitchen. He hollered back to me, "Dinner's ready."

I haven't experienced being nervous in so long, I almost forgot how it felt. I'm the one who is mostly in charge and in control. I'm usually the hard ass, but right now I'm as soft as a baby's bottom. Upon entering the kitchen, the table was set romantically. My table set didn't look the same. It has never had the appearance of elegance and sex at the same time. He had a white tablecloth on the table with red tiebacks for the chairs, along with red and yellow rose petals sprinkled here and there on the tablecloth. A medium vase of yellow, white and red roses, gold utensils and plates matched the wine glasses.

To top it off, there were red napkins and white plates trimmed in gold. I didn't know what to think. I'm being seduced in my own home, by a man I barely know, and I like it. Cooley had the food on a stand as he pulled out my chair. He fixed our plates and poured more wine. Seconds later, he sat in front of me. I was about to eat, but something told me not to. He touched my hands, and I swore I felt a high voltage flow through my body. Touching my inner palm with his thumb, he prayed for the food.

I'm still at wonderment about all of this. My words could barely come out my mouth as I said, "The food looks very inviting."

"It is. I used to cook all the time. I haven't done much of it lately and this morning, cooking for you crossed my mind."

"Honestly, this has never happened before and generally, no man has been in here but you."

"You don't entertain company at all?"

"I do, just not in my house."

"Glad you let me be your first."

"Glad you are too."

He has a bad habit of making me blush and it was unusual for me to be feeling like this and to be in a predicament I can't escape. Deciding to remove the attention from me, I asked, "What made you think I was at home or didn't have a man over?"

"I didn't know if you were at home and as for a man, I wasn't worried."

Strong; I like it, I thought, as I ate. I noticed he watched me, and I tried to pretend that I didn't notice, but I did. I couldn't help telling him, "You make me nervous for some reason."

"Don't be nervous, Catherine. Be you."

"Right now, I find it hard to be me. I mean, I'm always me, but to be caught off guard doesn't happen to me."

"Be prepared for a lot of caught off guard moments."

Here I go again, blushing and acting like I'm in school or something. This man is working me and doesn't know how fond he is making me of him. He is doing something to me and thinking sexually has never crossed my mind, which strikes me as odd. Cooley is most definitely a keeper, if I want to play in his field. I decided to make casual conversation by asking,

"You plan to stay around for a while or you in and out like the rest?"

"Depends on who you call the rest?"

"Investigators of course."

He sat back and asked me a serious question, "Do you want me around, or do you want me to be in and out like the rest?"

"If you like, you can stay around."

"That isn't what I asked you."

"Then yes; you have potential to be a great officer."

Cooley must have liked it, because he smiled. Time rolled by so fast and soon, he and I had cleaned up the kitchen and were in the living room watching a movie and eating popcorn. I've never done this with anyone before. I was delighting myself in his company. No way would I have believed it, but here I am in my own house, with a very attractive man. He came out to say, "I would like you to meet me in church."

The first thing came to my mind was, "I don't have time to go to church much."

"You have time to do everything else, why not give the man that loves you some of your time?"

Giving him a test, I questioned, "Tell me one reason why I should go to church, and I may consider it?"

146

"Sometimes you have things you go through, and you feel like no one understands, right?"

"Right."

"Why not cast all your cares upon the man who cares for you? Why not let *him* handle everything that is bothering you, or stopping you for being a better you? You see everyone is looking for something, why not let Christ be the one to seek?"

I was captivated by the words he just spoke, and it was like he was speaking directly to me to come to service. He must have realized he won, as he spoke, "Well?"

"You right. I will consider service with you, if I don't have to work."

"Great. Catherine, it's getting late, and I have a little boy to go home to."

"I didn't pay any attention about the time running away."

"You were having a good time, that's why."

He stood up and I stood up with him. I didn't know what to expect, because he was being such a gentleman. He waited at the front door as I handed him his roller cart and said, "I really was having a wonderful time. Thank you for coming by."

147

"We can pick this up tomorrow night at your mom's dinner."

"You going?"

"Yes, she said I became family when I joined the squad."

"See you then, good night."

"Good night."

He gave me a hug that had a profound sensation upon my body. I never knew a man's touch could do this to me. It wasn't sexual, but fascinating. Locking the door behind him, I had a smile on my face, the Joker couldn't even wipe off. Cooley has altered my life, and I don't know just how much. The bed had never felt so good to me; I went to sleep and slept all night long.

I awakened fresh and happy. My joyful emotion caused me to stop in the mirror and gaze. Placing my hair in a ponytail, I got dressed. Turning on the alarm, I locked the door and went to feed Beast. Deciding on my attire, I stretched, hooked Beast's roller collar up and we went jogging. This time we went towards momma's house. Who would've thought jogging would do wonders to a soul? I didn't. Beast and I made it to my mom's house very fast. She wasn't there. I stretched a few minutes, and we took back out towards home.

Cars were passing and blowing as their way of speaking. I waved back cheerfully and kept my pace. We arrived back home, and I tied Beast up after giving him some water. I stretched and unlocked the door. Turning off the alarm, I locked the door behind me and began stripping off. Headed straight for the shower, I allow the water to cover me completely. With my eyes closed, I could visually see Cooley gently washing my back and making me feel loved.

Suddenly, I opened my eyes and lay back against the wall. It hit me. Was I falling for him after being in his presence a brief period? Just being near him makes me feel different and I realized it instantly. Getting out the shower, I dried off and placed a towel about me. Straight to the kitchen I warmed up two slices of pizza and opened a can of Coke. I haven't been eating lately and that is weird. I know Cooley is going to be there and I need to wear something that gives me the essence

of a good girl.

I curled my hair in a lot of Shirley Temple curls. I didn't put on any makeup because I remembered what he said about makeup. Quickly, I dismissed it and added the Mad About You perfumed lotion all on my body. Making my way to the closet, I picked out a short, two-piece skirt set and boots. Turning the alarm back on, I locked the door and got in my truck. The drive to Momma's was shorter than usual. I saw Jarissa's car already there. Parking in the back, I went in through the back door.

Lo and behold, Cooley was in the kitchen with Jarissa. They looked surprised to see me. She was standing all under him as if his loving arms were holding her. My girl spoke first, "What's up, cuzzo?"

In a smug manner, I replied, "Looks like you got it."

"Naw, you got it," she said with a smile.

"Naw, you got it," I replied with a grin.

Walking towards me, Cooley said, "Hey, Catherine, it's good to see you."

"Is it?" I responded in a defensive manner.

"Yes, I was just telling Bell today how glad I was you aren't the type of woman to play games."

"I don't, but since you want to play games, let me in, Coach."

"Ain't nobody playing games over here. Cooley and I are just friends," my cousin stated.

"So are we."

I gave a short fake smile as I walked past them. My head began to spin. What the hell did I just witness? I asked her if she wanted him and she told me no, but I come to my mom's and they're in the kitchen holding a private conversation. I can't believe this. I almost let my guard down and now look. I fell and caught some damn feelings. I made it to the living room and Jarissa would come over, trying to talk to me and I'd go talk to someone else. Even if they were boring me to death, I wasn't going to be left alone with either one of them. Not if I can help it.

My mother came out, looking wonderful as ever. She didn't look quite her age, but she was spectacular. I stayed away from them. I didn't hear Momma announce the arrival of her love interest. He walked in and stood about her height. His name is Stuart Seeding and he's of Indian descent. He greeted everyone and came towards me. His manner was charming when I heard him ask me, "How do you do, Catherine? I have heard so much about you."

"That's good. I haven't heard much of anything about you."

He formed a small frown as he said, "I hope we can get to know each other and be a happy family."

"I'm sure my mother would like that and because she would like that; I'm willing to give this a shot for her."

"May I have a hug?"

Leaning into him, he gave me a hug. Once the embrace was over, he stated, "I want to ask you for your mother's hand in marriage."

151

My mouth dropped. First, she may retire and now he wants to marry her. I actually thought Momma was just saying that, but it is for real. I stepped back and stated, "Listen, you already have her on the verge of retiring, and now you want to marry her?"

"I know this is so fast, but I do love her. I pray in time we become close."

"Why are you asking me?"

"You are her daughter and since I cannot ask her father, I decided to ask you. I'm an old traditionalist and I do believe in morals and values. It would mean a lot to me if you would say yes."

I didn't say a word. I walked off and pulled Bell by the arm. He knew something was up as he followed me outside. He spoke rashly, "What's up, Hell Cat? You pulled me outside to gossip and not Jarissa."

"How about he wants to marry my momma?"

"What's wrong with that?"

"Everything."

"Cat, she's way past the age of eighteen. That makes her grown and she is moving on with her life. Do you want her to pout over your dad forever?"

Bell gave me a hug because I felt like crying, and this is an emotion I seldom show or do. For a brief time, he held me and allowed me to linger my head upon his chest. Before he married his wife, we talked all the time but we both know how jealous his wife is; we don't talk personally as much, but we still work together and play around. My co-worker pulled back to say, "Cat, if that is what makes her happy, let her do it. Stand behind her and be there for her. Get your own life."

"You're right."

"So, what's the deal with you and Cooley?"

"There is no deal. We're just friends."

"You and Jackson are just friends."

I laughed because he and I are just friends. I spoke with a smile, "If you must know, he came over and cooked a small dinner for me and we talked."

"I know where your 'talking' can lead."

He made me smile when he said that. I went on to reply, "Yesterday, he was with me at my house and today, he is at my mom's house with my girl."

"He's probably just talking to her. You know they used to chop up the airwaves months ago?"

"I know they used to talk all the time."

"I don't think he was feeling her like that and when he found out she's on that white girl, it was a definite negative. Now, he counsels her more than anything; that I do know. And that is probably what he doing now, Cat. He might have seen her, or she told him she was about to go get her high on."

"Maybe."

"You know she is a junkie."

"Don't call her that."

"Why not, that's what it is. When people get on it like that, they want it more than air. Your girl isn't any different. I mean, I love her, and she does her job, but she is a junkie. Drugs are not helping her one bit. Isn't that what we call people when we pick them up repeatedly for doing things for the drugs they want? It's just a matter of time before she sells a child or two."

It was funny but I didn't laugh. I was quiet, because he was right. To ease the moment, he stated a valid point to me. "You need to stop babying her and tell her to get some rehab help. If you don't, this will ruin her and anyone attached to her, and I don't want to see you pulled down a damn hole because she couldn't get it together. You're grown like she is, but damn. Cat, when is enough; enough?"

"I'm going to talk to her later about it, but that may not be what she and Cooley were doing."

"You already have and how did it go?"

"Not too well, but what am I to do? She's grown like you said and she won't listen to me."

"Let her hit rock bottom is all I know. This is something she must fix for herself. You can tell her all day long about what she needs to do, but until she wants to do it for herself, you just wasting your breath and time."

CHAPTER 11

Bell usually keeps things to himself. I couldn't focus.
The last time this happened to me was at Jarissa's party and
Ve-Lo showed up with his main woman. Now, I show up at my
mom's party and my ride or die is doing the same thing. Just
then, distracting me were the words, "You good?"

"I guess so."

"No guessing. We work on a job where guessing is the
last thing you do."

I smiled and replied, "Bell, I'm good. You good?"

"I'll be good later. Let's go back to the party. I'm ready
to eat."

We walked back through the door and Cooley was
staring at us. Jarissa was still on his hip, and I wasn't going to
let that get to me. She knows how we play and for now, I'll let
her think she's playing alone. Momma summoned us to come
to the table. Bell and Jackson practically ran as I grabbed a
chair between them, while Cooley sat between Renee and
Jarissa. I kept my eyes off him, but I could feel his eyes on me.
My mom stood as she said loudly and proudly, "Everyone, if
you are here, it is because I believe you to be family. I know
this is of short notice to some of you, but right to the point. I'm
getting married."

All my close co-workers were happy. They all got up, giving Mom her congrats. I did too, just to keep face. Each time Cooley came close to me, I would walk off. Finally, Jarissa pulled me off and said, "Girl, we just friends."

"Jarissa, we just family," I stated as I sized her up and down.

"He feeling you."

"And?"

"He saw me doing my thang and he was talking to me about it."

"We can talk later. Come by and chill with me."

"When? For the next two days you work, I don't and vice versa."

"I'll come early. I ain't got nothing else to do."

"Bet."

"Bet."

Soon as I made it home, I had a visitor in my yard. I got out and asked, "What you doing here?"

"I came to see you. I hadn't had you in a minute. From how you looking now and smelling, it brings back old memories."

"Put those old memories to bed and sleep on them."

"I can't. I need some Cat to make me sleep good tonight."

157

"My cat or any cat?"

"Your Cat."

He knows once he has me thinking, the next question is easy, and he asked it. "Where we going?"

"Let's go in my house," I said, surprised I even brought that up.

I opened the gate, and he drove in behind me. He parked his truck on the back as I went in, turned the alarm off and waited for him. Without locking the door, he rushed me with powerful kisses and massive hand touches. It has been a while since I had any man inside me and right now, I don't care who he belongs to. I could only think of Cooley with Jarissa; regardless of what he told me.

We didn't make it to my bedroom. He took me on the floor halfway between the living room and kitchen. It had been so long; I was enjoying the way he was taking me. I don't know what had gotten into him, but right now he is inside me. For hours on end, we had sex off and on between breaks. In my wildest dreams, I never knew him to be such a handful and aggressive. It didn't matter, I needed someone to help ease my mind from everything and he was doing it. Around four o'clock, I woke up and he was still there, lying beside me asleep. I reached over and thought about how he was supposed to have been my husband.

If he had been my husband, he wouldn't be laying up having sex with someone else. Feeling the need to have him again, I woke him up doing things my way. It didn't take long to get him aroused and it didn't take long to knock him back out. The more I watched O.B. sleep, the more I thought about my life. My mom has started her life and here I'm young and still unattached. O.B. woke up and saw me staring at him. He got off the floor and got on his knees in front of me. This man is so wonderfully made, and I care about him, but I believe those feelings are changing.

Placing my hands on each side of his shoulder, he stared into my eyes and spoke. "You know I could never leave you alone. No matter who I'm with, there is something about you that keeps me coming back. It's not just the sex, it's your entire personality. You make me laugh and you are fun to be around when we are with each other."

"But you must leave me alone."

Pushing his face inches from mine, he questioned me intensively, "What is wrong with what we are doing? What's wrong with being pleased by a woman you care so much for? Huh, tell me? What makes what we doing so wrong that we can't be together?"

"You need to ask those questions? You honestly don't know what is wrong with what we are doing? When we do this three out of four days a week and we are together a lot."

He dropped his head and pulled himself close to me. This moment is too perfect, but I broke it up to say, "I have to get involved in a relationship. I have to change my priorities and the way I live."

My love, my friend lifted his head back just enough for him to stare into my face, as he asked with his heart "Why you gone do that for? You know I care too damn much about you to see you with another. You mean so much to me and I always hoped we would make this official and move away from here. It could be the two of us, with no worries and no one to follow us."

"We talked about that before you did what you did. Do you have any idea how hard it was to pretend you didn't matter to me? It took everything I had. It was worse than my breakup with Ve-Lo and you know how it rocked my world."

"Do you know how hard it was for me to see you and not have you?" O.B. professed.

"I don't know about all that, but I do know the only way to get you out my system and get on with my life, is to leave you alone. It's not about you and me anymore. It's about me falling in love and staying in love. I've let you take up a lot of time in my life as is."

"Who's the lucky man I'm in competition with?"

"Why? You already have a woman in your life. If anything, I already have competition that I could smash at any time."

"I just want to know. Since you want to stop fucking me, I want to know who the guy is."

"And why?"

"I care a lot for you, Catherine, and who you want to see is important to me."

I was quiet as he said, "Is it Cooley, the guy you been working with, or is it Texan? Those are the only men in your life we have ever talked about."

"I don't know, but when I know, you'll know."

He laid his head back onto my breast and cried. I knew he would be hurt because we have been so close to each other, and most of the time we talked about my work, his work, or life in general. We were more like best friends than anything and we kept it real with each other. I knew what to expect and so did he. Even my eyes became watery as I listened to him sob about us leaving each other alone.

After crying for almost twenty minutes, he asked me with his heart in his hand, "Is that what you really want?"

"It's not what I want, it's what I believe will be best for me. I must start doing right. Don't you know we are held accountable for our sins? For the things we do wrong."

"You mean, not being with me anymore like this is what you really want? What about us talking about everything? No more of that either? Tell me, Cat. You just don't pull a man's heart out his chest and don't tell him anything more than what you have said."

"Don't I deserve to be happy?"

"You don't think I can make you happy?"

"I'm sorry, we have to do what is best for us, and if not talking to you on a personal level is what it takes, then so be it. I should get myself together and start thinking about my future, my life. You already have someone you go home to every night and day. Here at my house, it is only me. I'm alone and I've decided I don't want to be that way anymore."

He got up, dried his eyes, put his clothes on and didn't say anything else to me. It pained me in some form, but I should leave O.B. alone. Ever since Cooley has been in my life, he has been pushing me to do things with my life. He provokes me to good works and that is something no man has done since my dad's passing. He would make me laugh and he even talked to my mom about letting me go on drug raids. He has truly shown me he has the power of persuasion, which works.

Over the next few months, I spent a lot of undercover nights with Cooley. He even has me in church. I'm learning and I like it; to me that says something. When I don't understand something, he tries to make it plain and, in the end, I understand what the meaning is. This life Renee used to talk about isn't what I expected. It is better than I expected. I have found it hard to stop doing things, but I keep trying. Cooley and I would sit side by side at service and even hold hands.

He and I would laugh over silly stuff and have disagreements over petty stuff. From time to time, our discussions would be about what we wanted in life and where we saw ourselves. Basically, we talked about anything and everything; like friends do, but more personal. Cooley would teach me how to do investigations properly, which are way different than you learn in any textbook. He would tell me, experience is the best teacher, and he was right. This line of work has its perks, but it wasn't like the rush you get when you kick a door in, or you handcuff someone.

It is the safe job my mom wanted, but it is still rewarding, as I needed it to be. Everyone at headquarters was assuming that Cooley and I were a couple or something of a sort. We are taking it day by day and playing it by ear. We went out on many dates and spent much quality time together, but no sex. We were acting the part, and I was waiting on him to take it to the next step, because I know how I'm feeling him. I must be patient and let things happen.

However, he would often tell me the next woman he takes will be someone he can be with and how he doesn't like jumping in and out of women's beds. He has a son and clearly lets me know how he must be an example of what a man is like. We worked together and much of our conversations involved the job, but the rest involved us and his son. The parts that involved us were profound and emotional, beyond any that I have known. He gets me to open up and I discovered who I'm really without the badge to hide behind.

I never knew I had a problem with commitment until it came out. I had been learning so much from him and because of him, I'm thankful. I'm in the progress of expressing myself in a positive way and in that process; I do believe I'm falling in love with Cooley. Right when I was about to daydream, we got a call about a stolen, gray and green looking Buick Regal car running cars off the road. Jackson was writing up a report and Cooley was taking notes.

Bell and I took out in the patrol car to catch this drunk driver. Before we made it to Beulah Road by the water tank, we saw the car. I radioed that we have visual. With our lights flashing and sirens going, the car pulled over by King Road in Steele-Town. Bell drew his weapon as I asked the driver to get out the car with his hands up.

The driver got out slowly and raised his hands as he spoke, "See, I ain't got a thang on me but a dick in my pants, lady."

"Turn around and walk backwards before it's blown away."

The driver mumbled as he turned around. Something was odd about the passenger. I commanded the passenger to get out slowly and he started to get out. Suddenly, the driver fell, and Bell began to walk towards him with his gun back in his hostler. I took my eyes off the driver for one moment and the next thing I know, the passenger opened up and fired shots. The driver jumped up and ran back towards the car. Bell grabbed the driver, but the passenger shot rounds through the glass at Bell; causing him to let go of the driver and take cover.

Bell took out his gun and shot at the car numerous of times, as they drove off down Highway 21 towards Sebastopol. He used the radio on him to call for backup as he gave them our position. Bell ran over to me. From out of nowhere, the other two Scott County Boys were in a chase towards the mystery car. As I lay on the ground, my partner ripped off my uniform shirt. There in the chest were two shots, about seven inches apart. Luckily, I had on my bulletproof vest. Bell sat there and held me as if I were dying. He glared down at me. He could only say, "Cat. Cat."

I'm so grateful my police family care so much about me. He didn't even see if the slugs went all the way through. I finally got my wind back and mumbled, "Those slugs knocked the breath out of me, but I'll be ok."

"Let me take you to the hospital, Cat."

"No, I'm okay, really."

"It's protocol to go to the hospital and you know it."

"I know," I replied.

Moments later, he helped me up and opened the passenger side door for me. It was like my life flashed in front of me. I could only hear the shots, before being knocked down by the bullets. For the first time, I spoke out loud, "Thank you, Lord."

"You sure you don't need to go to the hospital?"

"Yeah, I'm sure."

"You know it is protocol," he said again.

"Make sure you put it in your report that I refused medical attention."

He turned his head and drove towards Forest. After riding for ten minutes, Bell looked over at me and continued driving me back to the station. Soon as I got there, everyone was there. All I could hear in my ear is my mother's voice, sounding frantic. I wish I could keep this from her, but I know I can't, too many mouths.

I had to give Bell my statement as I saw my mom's text. I only replied I was fine, and I had on my vest. Deciding to turn off the phone, I told Bell he needed to hurry up. He finished doing his part and left out to take another call. I took the rest of the night off and right when I was about to leave, I got a message from Renee to stop by Jarissa's. This caused me to be delayed a few more as Renee and I talked.

After being shot, things come to your mind and how you live your life is the top of the list. I walked out the door and saw my truck windshield busted. I screamed loudly, "What the hell!"

Like lightning, I ran back into the station and got other cops outside. I didn't go by my truck, because I know the first thing you do is get a witness and not to touch anything. Everyone came outside and saw it. One of the day cops had me to make a report as the other one took pictures. Things were crazy and everyone wanted to know like I wanted to know, who did it? Not only did I get shot, but someone did damage to my vehicle.

There was no message, but a cement block was properly tagged for evidence. I got some of the trustees to clean out my vehicle as I thought long and hard. I must make sure it was them and not a fluke. Seconds later, Bell and Jackson pulled up because it was clock-out time for them. They saw the commotion and boy; I hate they did. They always show up, when I don't want them to.

Getting out the car was Jackson. The first thing he said was, "Ok, dynamite, who have you pissed off now? Hurry up and think about it. The list is ten-yardsticks long and we really don't have all night to figure out, who you have wronged."

"I haven't done anything."

Bell pulled back up and added, "You must have done something."

"Bell, you know she won't tell it. She'll wait and do something. When she does, we'll know who it is."

"Jackson, you will be amazed what boys do these days when you push on."

"Yeah, they'll throw a cement block in your windshield," Bell added as they both laughed.

"It's funny now, but I thought you were on a call."

"I had a disturbance, but they canceled it, so I came back to the station."

"Cat, it isn't funny. You have a lot of frenemies, and it could be a list of people," Jackson added too.

"Go clock out and goodbye, Jackson."

The Scott County Boys left as I finished up filing an incident paper. I also called Alfa my insurance company. They set things up for me to rent a car at U-Save. One of the day shift officers dropped me off. They didn't have anything like my truck and that was a disappointment. Tomorrow, the glass company will pick my truck up from headquarters and repair the windshield. Right now, I have a bitch to call. Soon as I got in the vehicle, I called O.B. I didn't text. He picked up and I went off. "I know you did that to my truck."

"Really?"

"Now you going to pay for it and pay for this damn car rental."

"I can do that."

"Why the hell you do my windshield like that?"

"I heard you letting another man drive your truck."

"First, you don't pay anything on this end. Everything here says Catherine Roselita Le Beau. You lucky I don't press charges on you for doing that. Then, you destroy personal property on my job. Don't you know you can go to jail for that?"

"What the hell is jail, if I'm a prisoner without you?"

"You know what we said and what we're doing."

169

"I know what you said, I just couldn't hear it. Besides, that doesn't mean I don't want you or need you in my life. Don't you know you are perfect with me?"

"You need that woman you with in your life, who is perfect for you, not me."

He was quiet as he asked, "Can I come stay the night?"

"Are you sick or do you need help? You know where I park and you busted my windshield out, so why would I take you home and be with you?"

"Because I can make it good to you."

"Yes, you can, but what about my money for the damage you caused?"

"Get an estimate and get back with me."

"Later."

"Later."

I hung up and headed out towards the country. Soon as I got to Jarissa's she was sitting under her patio. She didn't look stoned, but it seems to be on the way. She stood up and said to me, "I didn't know who you were at first. Where is your truck?"

"Somebody busted the windshield."

"Damn. Who you piss off this time?"

"Why's everybody think I pissed somebody off?"

"Because you always do, Cat."

"Yeah, I do, don't I?"

"Yes. But I'm innocent today."

"They should have busted it when you were being naughty?"

"Right. Soon as I try to be nice, everything jumps off."

"What? You don't have Beast?"

"I just got off and Renee gave me your message, Jarissa. What's up?"

"Want some wine?"

"Yeah, might as well."

She handed me a bottle of wine as I sat in my usual seat and replied, "What's up?"

"It's all over headquarters that you fucking your way to the top."

"What the hell! That stank if I ever did smell anything that does."

"I told them you went to college and if you are, it's your business."

"You know that's bullshit."

"I know it and you know it, but you know how jealous people are."

"How could I possibly sleep my way to the top, if my mom is at the top? What, I'm fucking my mother?"

We let out a hearty laugh at that as we drank more. I had to make a point by telling her, "You need to tell those bitches and sons of bitches, to mind their own business and stay the hell out of mine, because getting in my business will make me give them the business."

My best friend laughed at me, and I drank some more wine. Looking as serious as ever, my girl sat back and stated, "I wish I could redo my life over and be better."

"I've learned since going to church we can't change the past, but we can do better in our future. The Lord wants us to surrender ourselves to *him* and *he* won't make us do what we don't want to do. He gives us the free will and it's up to us to choose *him*."

"Sounds like you are listening to Cooley."

"Some of it I am, but mostly from experience and the pastor at the church."

"You always had it made."

"How?"

"You grew up with your parents, Cat."

"And you grew up with my parents too and a sister. You know my parents were like y'all parents as much as they were mine."

"No, I grew up with your parents, who happens to be my aunt and uncle."

"It doesn't matter; you were there like I was. They never made you feel any less. If they did, I never saw it."

"But it's not the same. You got all the lucky breaks."

"How? I joined the girls in blue because of the ruthless attitude I got from Ve-Lo. I'm the daughter of the captain of police and I fell for a top-notch drug dealer."

"Your attitude makes up for what you lack, and I was always your shadow."

"You are my best friend. I love you and the sky is the limit. If something is wrong, talk to me."

"I don't want you feeling a certain way and not express yourself."

"It's nothing really. I just wish you the best in life."

"What do you call the best?" I asked as I drank some more wine.

"Cooley."

"What about him?"

She said, "I want things to work out for you both. I really do. He's a good guy and you ok."

"Oh, I'm just ok."

"You'll do."

She laughed and realized I missed hanging out with her but my job causes me to just text and call only. She laid her head back. Slowly she raised it up to say, "I don't want you to

173

end up alone like me and being a single parent. It's a struggle and if the opportunity presents itself and your children need it; you'll do whatever it takes to get it."

"How are you alone when we all love you?"

"I don't have a man and I'm not stable. This habit I have is getting me into something deep and I can't back my way out the rabbit hole."

"Talk to me. You would tell me if you were in trouble or thinking about doing something stupid, right?"

"Yeah, I would."

"Jarissa?" I added more earnestly.

"Yeah, I'll tell you if I don't tell anyone. You and I have done some stupid things together and we have been there for each other. But there are things I want to say, need to say but can't."

"Yes, you can say anything you want to me. You know I will listen, and I won't judge you for the world."

"That's what I love about you, Cat. You never looked down your nose at me and you have always been the one faithful friend I'm glad to know. It's been me thinking you supposed to be snobby, but you really aren't. No matter how much I say you have it made you never acted like it. You would act as if you were broker than the next man. You never let money or drugs get to you. Cat, you always kept a level head, and I guess I admired that about you more than I wanted to let on."

She cleaned off a spot on the glass table and I know what she is about to do. Trying to distract her I asked, "What you say about Cooley and me?"

She stopped for a second and replied, "I asked how things with you and Cooley?"

"We ok, just doing a job like always."

"I'm glad for you both; I really am, because I wouldn't make a good woman for him. At least, you have a chance to be a wife."

"You do too."

"No, I'm on drugs with no quitting in sight. For now, this white dope is my husband. She makes me do things I don't care to do and when I need her, nothing matters. I sound like a junkie, don't I?"

"You sound as if you need help but won't ask for it."

"I do."

"If you don't want to do a rehab, remember Jesus still saves and *he* still heals. Come to church, you may like it; I do." She gave me a short smile as I made my claim to her, "I love you, Jarissa. You have been a sister to me like no one has."

"I feel the same way."

CHAPTER 12

We were quiet as we drank some more. I don't know where it came from, but Jarissa sat up and said, "Texan asked about you."

"Where you see him at?"

"Must you ask where I have seen him at?"

"When did you see him?"

"About ten minutes before you showed up."

She took out the white capsule. I humped my shoulders, to say that I didn't care that she has seen him and that he asked about me. Feeling sleep come over me I asked, "Is that all you have to tell me? I should be getting home. I have to do drills with Beast and work tomorrow."

"Yeah, that is all."

We hugged and I drove off towards home. Soon as I made it to my gate, I got a call.

"O.B., why are you calling me?"

"I want to see you."

"See me later. I have work tomorrow."

"I want to come by and help you go to sleep."

"I don't need you for that."

"Come on, Cat. You know that I can make it good to you. I can do it just the way you like it."

Now, I'm thinking, about how he can really do that and so much more. Wiggling my legs, I smiled as he asked again, "Well, you gonna let me come pet the cat three ways?"

"Just this once. You lucky I work night shift, and I haven't started sleeping with him yet."

"You don't have anything to worry about. I'm sure you and he are not close to being serious."

"Why you say that?"

"If he wants to be serious with you, he would've made you his by now."

Not wanting to hear about the man I'm after, I rerouted the conversation to say, "I just made it home. What time will you be here?"

"Give me thirty minutes."

Placing my cell on silent, I unlocked the gate and parked the rental. Going straight to Beast, I fed him dog food and poured him fresh water. He was super excited to see me. I admit I missed him too, because we went everywhere together and have worked cases together. It hit me. I'd rather do K-9. Deciding to permit Beast to wonder the gated yard, I unlocked the door.

Turned off the alarm and locked the door back. As if nothing changed, I began stripping out my uniform and placed them on the edge of the couch. I straightway aimed for the shower. Soon as the water rushed me, I heard a horn blowing. Cutting my shower short, I snatched my robe and went to the front door. It was Cooley. He turned off the ignition and lights. I called out, "Beast, stand down."

Beast got in his stance as Cooley came straight at me. At that precise moment, a car pulled into my driveway. I didn't know what to think. They kept their lights on bright, but I knew automatically who it was and why they were coming. Cooley looked back at the car and asked, "Who is that?"

"I don't know. It might be just turning around," I spoke hastily.

"It looks like one of our old, unmarked cars that were sold to the public," Cooley added.

"Can't be Jackson or Bell. They probably sent someone out here to check on me, being nosey," I spoke because I didn't want to know who it was.

"Oh, may I come in?"

I stood to the side and watched him come in. The car continued to stay there. I guess they'll have something to pick at me about. I closed the door and locked it. Soon as I turned around, Cooley kissed me feverishly. He caught me off guard with this. I didn't know how to react at first, but the woman in me woke up and kissed him back just as passionately

Cooley swooped me up while keeping his lips on me. I can't believe he is here, doing this to me as he laid me on the couch.

"No, take me to my bed."

He carried me to my bedroom as if I were his bride on our honeymoon. Being careful, he laid me upon the cool comforter. Pulling back, he announced, "I'm falling in love with you and in my mind, I state that you are just a dear friend to me, but my heart and body knows it's not so. Allow me to take you as the first woman I've had since the departing of my wife."

I didn't have to say yes; my body was saying it for me. Cooley removed my robe and before him was my cool body, still damp from the water. He sounded sexy when he said to me, "I love the way you look out of uniform and every time I'm alone with you, I don't want you to cover up. I can't stop looking at you."

"Be quiet and kiss me."

Cooley did just that. All night, he and made love and it was like no other. He was like a skilled craftsman, perfecting a work of art. He was making an ordinary piece of wood out of something marvelous. In all my days, no one has ever made me feel this way. Cooley took his time to take me, and he took his time in showing me how a man makes love to a woman. I felt so alive and so joyful. I never knew lovemaking could be so passionate and so awakening to a woman like me.

For hours on end, I couldn't keep my hands off him; just being in this king-size bed alone with him made me dizzy with anticipation of him. I didn't think about how tired and sleepy I was, because I was being loved by a man who wants me for me. Nothing could disturb this moment, and I wasn't going to let anyone take this away from me. When I awoke, Cooley was up. I heard him rambling, so I went to see what the racket was all about. He was in the kitchen cooking me breakfast. This is another first.

Smiling, I walked behind him with my short arms and held him. This feels so right. I now know why when women fall in love they fall out of line, because if the man is as good as Cooley is to me; you can't help it. He touched my hands and romantically said to me, "Good morning, my love. I mean, evening, but morning to us."

"Good morning and evening to you too."

"You had me worried."

"You know this is a worry type of job, and I knew it when I signed up for it."

He gave me a look that I can't describe as he changed the subject. "I'm cooking you a small breakfast. I hope you like it."

"I'm sure I will because it is done by the man who loves me."

He turned around and kissed me. I don't understand how I can get so heated up from his touch alone, but I did. Cooley is bringing things out of me I thought was never there. He pulled back some and stated with fever, "You better stop before you have more than the breakfast I'm cooking."

"I can handle that."

I went back into my room. I checked my cell and saw that O.B. blew my phone up last night with calls and texts. I saw he texted me over one hundred times. I opened his first few texts.

O.B.: *I know you not giving him the business, when it's supposed to be me.*

O.B.: *What you doing that you can't answer your phone or text me back!!*

O.B.: *You don't want me angry.*

Closing the phone up, I jumped in the shower. The water felt good upon my skin as I closed my eyes to remember how lovely the night was last night with Cooley. I can't stop smiling and this feels so right; my life is feeling complete. Now, all I should do is to admit it to him how I feel and not care what others think. I got out the shower and put on a new set of pajamas. Soon as I walked out the room, he had the table set.

Cooley had a huge smile as tall as he was when I said to him, "This is fit for a queen."

"You are my queen, and I plan to show you."

I walked towards the table, and he pulled my chair out. I already knew, but I had to ask, "Are you always going to be doing this for me, or is this a ploy to wrap me in your web?"

"A man is a gentleman, and I will aim to do so at all times."

As we sat down, we prayed and began eating the delicious breakfast he had prepared. Our conversation was light and hearty. I hadn't laughed this much in a long time and it's all because of the man across from me. My dad would be so proud of me, if he could see the kind of man I have in my life right now. Breaking my thoughts, Cooley asked, "Do you think you can ever love me?"

"Yes, why wouldn't I?"

"I just want to know what your take is on what we have."

"I take it that we are going out and going to see where this relationship leads."

"I like the sound of that."

When the evening breakfast was over, we fed Beast and did some tactics with him. We had fun being outside and when I told him about wanting to join the K-9 Unit, he was happy for me. He didn't think that it was stupid going from being a patrol officer, to investigator to now K-9. That is one thing I like about being with Cooley, he listens to my ideas, and he takes them seriously by pushing me to greatness. He has yet to say how foolish something sounds or how whack something was.

He would listen and question me to see if I really wanted what it was, I was asking. After we put Beast up, he made a comment, "If I don't leave to let you get ready for work, we both will be calling in and police work will be the last thing on my mind."

I kissed him back and used warm words when I spoke. "I have plenty of vacation time I don't mind using. But you know like I know, the people on our jobs are watching us like they are the FBI or the feds."

Cooley gave me a hearty kiss and a loving squeeze as he left out. It was getting late, and I know we have to get ready for work. I got ready with glee. Turning on the alarm and locking the door, I headed off to work. Soon as I got there, I should have known something was up. O.B. had his car parked out front of the station. Paying it no mind, I saw my truck was gone as I parked the rental. Before I could go inside, O.B. called me out front, "Let me holler at you for a minute."

He was standing on the other side of the door as I waved at Renee and walked towards O.B., wondering what he could possibly want. He appeared anxious, nervous even. I hollered out, "Let me clock in."

I clocked in and came back out front where he was waiting, to ask impatiently, "What is it?"

"Let's go this way."

Leading me towards the old driver's license room, we went inside. He snapped, "What the hell was he doing at your house?"

"It's none of your business, but if you must know, he showed up unexpected."

"He doesn't need to be doing that."

"He's trying to be my man, why not? I don't have anything to hide."

"What you call this? What do you call what we been doing off and on for over three years now?'

"Having fun without commitment?"

"I stand to lose it all and you are worth more than just fun to me."

"What you want?"

"I want you. I got to have you."

"When?"

"Now. I need to feel you."

"I'm at work and I'm clocked in on company's time. You know that, plus we are not messing around on that level."

"Don't you see I don't give a damn anymore? You are all that matters to me. I'll risk it all just to be with you. I bring you the excitement you need and miss. With him, he's a more on the safe side kind of guy, while me; I bring you the adrenaline rush that I know you require so much."

"What if I'm not into that, like I used to be?"

"Take off that gun belt and pants. Show me you don't like this thrill I bring you."

Quickly without thinking, I took off my gun belt and pants. In haste, O.B. took me in the dark room against the wall. It was wild, crazy and exciting. I loved it, just like he knew I would. Soon as he finished, he kept holding me as if I were his baby in the air, still hung inside me. After a few more moments, he gathered his breath and put me down. He stared down at me to say, "Good, wasn't it?"

"You know it was. It's always good and I can't lie. You know how to bring out the kinky girl in me."

He handed me a soapy wet towel. *He must've had this planned.* As he got dressed, I was putting on my shoes. From the blind side, he stated, "Cat, I have a solution."

"To what?" I asked as I tied up my shoes.

"Being with you."

"And what is it?"

I looked up at him soon as I finished tying my shoes. With a scary face and a strong voice, he stated directly to my face, "If you don't quit seeing your friend, I may have to go on and kill my woman."

He closed the door, and my feet would not sustain me. They became weak as I grabbed the seat my feet were once on. I can't believe he just walked in the police station, of all places, and said what he just said. I know O.B. and I know he would do it because he means it. He never states anything like that if he doesn't mean it. I trembled as my clothes found my body in haste. My breath was nowhere to be found. I had to get out the station.

I need to get away. Coming out the room, I saw Cooley. The puzzled appearance on his face was noticeable. Doing my best not to let it get to me, he grabbed me by the arm. I jerked away and kept moving. At this point, we are in the middle headquarters. Jackson and Bell are at their desks, getting prepared to do a roadblock. The nerves in my body continued to make me move rapidly. I know I must make a scene, and it must be a real one. Trying to think of something to front about, the opportunity came when Cooley walked behind me and asked nicely, "Cat, what is wrong with you? You seem distant."

"You. That's wrong with me. Can't you see I don't want you?"

I know that threw him off, because it threw me off. His being surprised is an understatement. He spoke, "Huh? What are you talking about? I'm completely lost, and I don't know what just happened."

"I'm talking about you and how I don't want you, and I'm damn sure not ready to be a step-momma to a fucking spoiled kid."

"Don't talk about my kid," he said as I touched a nerve.

"I'll talk about what the hell I want."

The look on his face was hurtful and ashamed. I know he doesn't know what I'm talking about, because we were just together, and he was telling me of his emotions. And now, here I am today ripping his heart out his chest and stomping on it for all to see. I would've given anything in the world not to do it to him, but if I don't and O.B. finds out I'm still seeing my friend, his woman is dead.

I can't and won't have her blood on my hands, even if I don't care for her. It's the principle of the matter. When I left her husband alone, I should not have started back. I had no idea this would go deeper than it was. The preacher was just talking about extramarital affairs. I didn't think it really applied to me, because I wasn't married, and we weren't doing it like that. Honestly, I really thought we could hit it and quit it like old times, but I was wrong.

The fact is cops know how to cover up for each other. We spend all our time helping the grateful and ungrateful. It's only right we take up for one of our own. It's a secret society we defend for the badge, and we protect those who wear it as best as we can. I haven't had to lie or do anything of that nature, but I know of those who have and if push comes to shove, I might; just like I'm doing now.

Cooley continued to stand there. I got all up in his private space to say, "You heard it right. I never wanted you. I only wanted to see if I could get you and I could. Now, I've been there done that, next yourself."

He still stared at me as Jackson and Bell stared and gawked. I pushed him and he fell backwards. To ridicule him, I added, "What, you fell in your feelings?"

It was too much to see. On the inside, I was crying because I didn't want to do that to him. I had fallen for him and to know I'm hurting him broke my heart.

I walked off and spoke with a joke to play it off, "What y'all looking at?"

"We looking at dynamite explode," Jackson stated back.

"You couldn't do that to me," Bell stated as he and Jackson walked out the door.

Renee stood on top of the small steps glaring at me. I threw her the keys to the rental; in case they came with my truck. I could tell she is wondering what just happened. I walked out the door and got in my old patrol car. There was no way I was riding with Cooley after that scene I just pulled. About thirty minutes later, Renee dispatched, "Cat, you have a 10-22."

"10-4."

I was just riding around over dirt roads, wanting justification for what I did to Cooley, and none came to mind. It means, I would've to admit to sleeping with O.B. from time to time and I wasn't sure I wanted to do that. All in the back of my mind I heard the preacher say, "Sin and sinners go hand in hand; liars and whoremongers, robbers and thieves." Sighing, I didn't want to drive all the way back to Forest so I radioed her back, asking, "Who wants to see me?"

"10-9."

"Who wants to 10-22 me at the station?"

"Alfa insurance has returned your truck, and you need to sign something."

189

"I give you permission to sign it for me."

"10-4."

Across the CB, I heard Jackson and Bell responding to a 10-50. I wondered where the wreck was at because nothing is going on out here on this side of the country. I wonder what Cooley is doing. Then I remembered he doesn't want to talk to me. Personally, I don't blame him. I showed my ass and then told him all kinds of lies. The worst part was, I did it in front of our police family. I sighed as I cried. I couldn't believe I did this to the man I was falling for. I hadn't felt this way since Ve-Lo.

My tears would not stop as I let them out for a minute. I thought about Ve-Lo. I stopped crying and decided to take my frustrations out on someone; why not him, Texan or Texan's girl? Making my way towards the Golden Memorial Sate Park, I was like a hound on a hunt. I know the type of car they all be in or drive. I waited until I saw Texan's car at the Railroad Crossing store. Just as my mind knew it, he got in the car and took the road beside the store towards his home.

Finally, the break I needed came. *He has a busted taillight,* I thought. I wasn't going to let him get on the Park Road, so I hit my siren and lights, and he pulled over calmly. I got out the car and he saw that it was me. He gave me a cunning smile as I asked, "License, registration and proof of insurance."

"Cat, you know I'm covered, so tell me why'd you really stop me?"

"You have a busted taillight."

"I just ordered the part and it'll be here tomorrow."

He handed me the paper, which lined up to what he was saying. I smiled when he said to me in a cheesy way, "Officer Cat, what is it that you really want to know?"

"You tell me?"

"Maybe you want to know about where ya girl buys her new dope from."

"Why, my girl buying weak dope?"

Texan gave me a smile that showed all his gold teeth. Used to be a time when those gold teeth made me squirm but today, I want to sucker punch him in them. Tilting his head towards me, he said, "I'm going to tell you this, because you mean something to me. I don't do this for a lot of people, but I will for you."

"Do what?"

"Ya girl is strung out bad and she doesn't buy 'caine. She has upped her game to heroin and a touch of meth."

I felt like falling as I heard him tell me she is on a more powerful drug. I asked, pretending as if what he said didn't bother me much, "How you know?"

"She buys it from Ve-Lo and that's who she's been fucking."

"The one down by the tracks?"

"The same one you used to sleep with."

"I used to trick off with you, so why not you?"

"Because I turned her down. I told her I may be low down, but you were too important for me to mess over, money or not. Then she approached Ve-Lo, and he did it. The word on the streets says he's fucking the hell out of yo girl in all kinds of ways. He's making her suck his dick and his niggas' dicks and you know his group is scandalous and getting down with anyone."

The rain started falling lightly as I wanted to faint again. I needed to get out of the rain, but this blow has been a lot to hear. He came out and whispered, "You didn't think I knew?"

I didn't say a word as the rain came down a little harder. However, I was listening as he said, "I make it my business to keep up with your business. And to think, you mix business with pleasure."

Right when I was going to comment, a small blue S-10 pickup truck zoomed by. It caught my attention as I spat out loud, "What the hell?" When I heard the truck skid and crashed. I ran back to my patrol car and dispatched out, "I have a 10-50 on Golden Memorial State Park Road. Call for ambulance, 10-4?"

Leaving Texan, I took a right on the Golden Memorial State Park Road. A few feet away down a half-slanted hill, I saw the small frail truck. The rain had picked up momentum and making my visual hazy, but from what I could see here, the truck hit a tree on the passenger side. Making my way to the truck, I noticed the window was down and radiator smoke. Closer as I approached it, I noticed the driver was of the Caucasian descent with shoulder-length, blonde-like hair.

She appeared to be bleeding from the forehead and maybe unconscious. I made it to the door of the vehicle and the smell of liquor was everywhere. Quickly considering my inspection, the victim had the look of someone that had been in an altercation. Her hair was wet and clingy, and I didn't see anything that could cause me or her harm. I tried to open the door, but it was stuck. The young girl began moaning and moving her head hysterically. Sounding sincere, I called out to her, "Be still; you are hurt and the ambulance is on its way.

Ma'am, can you hear me? Help is on the way. You're going to be ok, just hang in there."

In a small childlike voice, she said, "No, let me die. I just want to die. Life isn't worth living anymore."

"Talk to me, ma'am. What is your name? Stay woke. Ma'am, talk to me by telling me your name."

She faced me with a lost look. Blood had entwined with the locks of curls, and she was sweating. I tried opening the door, but couldn't. The young girl licked her lips, and said, "He don't want me. He cheated. He cheated with my sister on me. They hurt me. They really hurt me."

"Ma'am don't worry about that right now. Let's get you out of here and get you safe, okay?"

"Let me die. Just let me die. I want to die. He doesn't love me no more."

"Ma'am, I can't do that. Hang on. I can hear the ambulance sirens."

Texan called behind me, "You need some help?"

I looked back and replied quickly, "Yes, I need to open the door, but it is stuck. Come help me!"

Facing the young girl, she cried as she said, "Tell Yu-Ti I love him, and this is what he did."

"I'll tell him, just hang on."

I turned my head because Texan's words exploded from him, "Move, let me try!"

No sooner than he said that a shot rang out. Jolting back, we saw the young girl had blown her brains out. I was stunned and Texan fell back on his hands. He just sat there bewitched. The ambulance arrived and so did the troopers. It was too late. She killed herself and I felt helpless. Nothing equipped me for what happened. I tried keeping her calm and I didn't see the weapon at all. When coming up on a scene or even stopping a car, you check for anything out of the ordinary and other than her appearance, nothing was different.

CHAPTER 13

Texan looked terrified and puzzled as the rest of us. We still had a job to do as we marked off the crime scene. With a few strong pulls, we got the door to open. Another officer called the coroner, and another one took our statement. I really can't believe this. Many emotions rushed me at once. I got in my car and dispatched in, "Dispatcher Renee, is Captain in route?"

"That is a negative. She won't be in until the day after tomorrow. 10-4?"

"10-4."

Driving slowly, Jackson called me on my personal cell. I didn't feel like talking, but I know I can always talk to him. I touched the answer key and heard, "You, okay? We overheard about what happened."

"I'm in shock."

"If we don't get a lot of calls, Bell and I will handle them. Right now, you need to go back to the station and play dispatcher for a while."

"I need to do something because this has messed me up for the rest of the night. She was so young and distraught over a man. She took her life over a man who cheated with her sister. I don't know her, but I know she had much more to live for, than to let a man be her downfall."

"You know this goes with the territory."

"I know, but I never had this to happen to me."

"I haven't either and I've been an officer longer than you and Bell put together. You know, Captain, may want you to go talk to someone. You just got shot and now witnessing something like that can mess with your thinker; plus, you know it is procedure."

"I know."

"What's your twenty now?"

"I'm in route back to the station."

"Ok. We're over here in Brusha and just left H-town. We had a 10-47."

"Whoever is acting up, take their ass to jail."

"Trust me, that's our intention. Then we might ride to Murrell-Town. There's never anything going on over there, but we have to make rounds."

"I used to ride that way to pass time."

"We do it too."

"Get at me later, Jackson."

"A'right."

I arrived back at the station and did my paperwork. This is the first fatality I ever had to do and to have witnessed it was another thing. Soon as I wrote out all the documentations, Cooley showed up. He gave me a hug, even after all the stuff I said to him in front of everyone. He stepped back a few feet and said, "I don't know why you did that to me and in front of everyone here. Right now, I'm not going to talk about us. You need someone to talk to about what you saw, and I'm here for you. We will talk about one thing at a time and right now, you need to get yourself together and don't let this bother you."

"Thank you, Cooley."

"Grab a seat up there with Renee and I'll help the rest of them patrol."

"Okay."

He kissed my forehead and walked out the station.

"If that man doesn't care about you, I don't know one that does," Renee said as she witnessed what happened.

"Renee, I've messed up and I don't know what to do."

"We have about five more hours before we get off. We can talk about it."

Going upstairs in her dispatch area was odd. I hadn't been in this office since my small time on day shift and then I didn't do anything. I grabbed a seat as she took the one in front of all the switches. She smiled as she teased, "Ok, I'm listening."

"I saw Cooley and Jarissa together and I felt weak. In fact, she was with Cooley all night, so I assumed he was feeling her and I was available to do anything I wanted. Unfortunately, it included doing O.B."

"Shut the front door!"

"I knew you had him before, but now after Cooley…"

"Let me explain."

"Yeah, please explain."

"It first started back before Cooley came. I was wilder and I like the way he makes my heartbeat fast with all his crazy ways to have sex. Any position, any time; he and I were on it and doing it as often as possible."

"Isn't he committed?"

"Yes, but I didn't think it was my problem since I wasn't married, but after listening to your preacher, I now know better."

"Right."

"Nevertheless, we were sleeping together but once I started talking to Cooley, I changed. I saw his change was good for me and I told O.B. I didn't want to see him anymore. Like I said, I only did it that night because I felt like Cooley had played me."

"I don't know why you did that. You know how competitive you and my sister can be sometimes. This isn't new to you, Cat."

"I know, but you remember I told her if she was feeling him to let me know, and I'd back off."

"She may not be feeling him like she told you."

"Why tell me to have a go, then I come to Momma's party and she's all over him. I guess the only thing is he's not married, and she likes married men."

"I understand what ya saying, but a committed man is still a committed man, nonetheless."

"I'm the main one who doesn't like committed men, because I don't have time for all the drama one can bring. But look what I did in a moment of weakness to one."

"Next time, take your own advice."

"You don't have to worry about a next time. Since that night after Momma's party, I told him I can't sleep with him anymore and I was hoping on a relationship with Cooley."

"How did he take it?"

"He cried like a baby at my house when I told him I didn't want him anymore. He would still talk to me when we saw each other, but he never let on anything different."

"I know! I never would've known you two were doing it again if you hadn't told me."

"All of this because my sister was all over a man that isn't into her? I mean, didn't you know you would be putting what you have accomplished with Cooley on the line?"

"How, when I thought he didn't want me? I was still ready from the night he came over and cooked. Being frank, I took it as my cue to start back doing me and to get out of my feelings."

"Sounds like you wanted to do you anyway; just needed an excuse."

"Maybe?"

"But what happened after we left that made you feel in dire need of a taken man?"

"Let's see, he cooked dinner. We cleaned up the kitchen, watched a movie and ate popcorn, talked about us and life. He didn't do anything sexually, but he had me wanting something sexual. Concentrating was hard because I wanted him, and he wasn't paying me any attention. All I could think about was him and me in the bed making love. I've been so busy working, that's when I remembered I hadn't had an orgasm since Texan and don't you know how long that has been?"

"It's been a while."

"I was amped and ready, but no good."

We laughed at that remark as I said, "That night, I was ready, and you know I love to have sex. Think about it; he got me all heated up and ready, but he wasn't in the state to close the deal. O.B. came over after I left the party and we did it off and on all night. You talking about good. Lord have mercy, I hadn't realized how long it had been since I had sex with a man inside of me. O.B. wouldn't go home, but before he did, I told him we can't do it anymore and until today, we hadn't."

"When today?"

"When he came in and called me to the old driver's license room."

"Wow."

"He's changed."

"He the one who broke your windshield, isn't he?"

"Yup. The crazy part is, he called me and wanted to come over and bring me the money. I told him to come over. Then unexpectedly, Cooley came over a few minutes before him."

"No way."

"Yes, Cooley was walking up to my door when O.B. came by."

"What did O.B. do?"

"He stayed in the driveway and watched Cooley go in the house."

202

"What'd Cooley come over for?"

"He came over just to make love to me and we did."

"Y'all finally, did it?" Renee said with delight.

"Yes, and it was magical, mystical, and all those words that are so surreal. He took his time to have me, and I loved it more and better than being with O.B."

"I'm so happy for you."

"Me too, but I've messed it up."

"Does Cooley know about O.B.?"

"No. I can't tell him, and I don't think I ever want to. I wish I could just keep it my secret and be done with it."

"You know bad things can't stay hidden for long."

"You are so right."

Renee got up and took a few calls out to the officers. She sat back down to ask, "What about your windshield? Does Cooley know that O.B. did it?"

"No, but O.B. gave me the money to get it fixed."

"That doesn't matter. If he breaks your windshield, be advised there is no telling what he may do."

"I know. He told me if I don't leave my friend alone, he is going to kill his woman."

Renee stared at me as if I were a blank sheet of paper. She was just as uneasy about it as I was when I heard it. To say it out loud, doesn't sound right at all. My dear cousin touched my hands and held them as her words came out, "I know you can take care of yourself, but when a man like that feels he has nothing to lose, there is no telling what he may do. Be advised that sounds like trouble or death."

"The tricky part is I believe him. I really do think he will do something to her, but he could be pulling my leg, just to get me single again."

"You have to tell Captain. If he goes through with it, he could say you told him to and you could get time for nothing."

"I know."

"That is why you did Cooley the way you did, isn't it?"

"I had to. If I hadn't, O.B. might do it but I don't really know. The crazy thing is I'm falling for Cooley like never before. As awesome as it may seem, I don't believe I can tell him what I had done."

"You have no choice."

"Honesty isn't always the best policy."

Remembering what I had to say from earlier, I said, "Let me switch the subject for a minute."

"What?"

"I talked to Texan."

"When?"

"He is the one I had pulled over right before that girl killed herself."

"Why was he pulled over?"

"A busted taillight."

"Cat, really? A busted taillight."

"He did have a busted taillight. I also told him not to have any dealing with your sister."

"What he say?"

"He said she's upgraded to heroin and she's sleeping with Ve-Lo and doing everything under the sun with him and his crew."

"Your Ve-Lo?"

"Yeah."

"You believe it?"

"Yeah."

"Why would you believe it without talking to her first?"

"I talked to her the other day, and she told me she is doing some things; you may not know like I know, but when someone is on drugs, they are not who they used to be. True, Jarissa is our loved one, but when she needs a hit and she can't get it, she'll do just about anything for it. And if sleeping with Ve-Lo is going to keep her supplied when she can't buy; then that's what she's going to do. Like it or not."

Renee knew I wasn't lying. She knows I would protect Jarissa with everything I have and for me to say something about her like that; it must have some truth. Renee looked

205

glossy eyed at me. I know she is on the verge of crying; I can see it in her eyes. She is emotional and I forgot she is pregnant. I can't imagine hearing about a real sister of mine on any drugs, but I had to tell her since I'm telling it all. Renee whispered lightly, "Heroin?"

"Yeah, that's what he told me."

"Cat, she can't afford such an expensive addiction."

"That's why she sleeps with the main supplier for it."

"You're going to ask her, aren't you?"

"You know I am. I don't know who my sister is anymore. How did this happen, and we didn't know it?"

"She would never let you see her, but me…I knew about the lightweight drugs, but this one is all new to me like it is to you."

"But heroin?"

"Renee, when she has her fix, she is the same Jarissa, and when she doesn't get her fix, we don't know her. Your preacher says to pray for people and that is what we must do in her case. We love her, but Jesus loves her more and it's up to *him* to save and fix her. As much as we want to, we can't do it. She told me the other day she knows she has a problem and wishes she could have done her life different."

She smiled as she said, "You do listen when you come to church."

"I told you that Cooley has been good for me, and I have changed more than I realized. I'm quoting scriptures and applying them to my life."

"I've noticed you haven't used any vulgar language."

"Thanks to Cooley. He has shown me a man can love a woman, even to her core."

"That is the type of love I have with my husband, and I'm so glad you are finally experiencing it for yourself."

"I guess the only way to fix it, is to tell him."

"Does the end justify the means?"

"When you down, you have no real friends, but soon as you get to standing, you have friends from everywhere. I guess so."

Suddenly, we both heard over the CB, "Shots fired, officer down."

Renee jumped on it to say, "What's your 20?"

It was Jackson's voice. "We are out in Murrell-Town. Call an ambulance."

Renee sprang into action and dispatched an ambulance to their location. I took off and Cooley stated, "Ride with me."

He and I got in the car. He raced through traffic faster and better than I would've as our lights blinked, and our siren roared. We didn't say a word as he drove to our fellow co-workers. The scene was hectic one. For as far as the eyes could see, there was grass on top of grass, and there in the middle of this field was a worn brick house. Jackson had Bell sitting up in the car at the end of the driveway. I was overwhelmed to see all this. Cooley and I went over to Bell with our guns drawn. He didn't say a word as he gave me that smile and passed out from the blood loss.

We knew the paramedics couldn't come in until the scene was secured; therefore, we easily moved Bell into a location that excluded them from harm's way. They loaded him up and took him off to the hospital. Other officers had arrived, and they too had their guns out.

Jackson stated, "We hadn't been down that way in a while and were checking it out, when a disturbed man yelled for us to get off his property. During that time, a woman ran outside, and he shot in the air for her to stop. She halted and we ordered him to drop his weapon. The woman had fear all about her as he took her back in the house. When Bell was getting back in the car, he shot and hit Bell right next to the vest."

The county negotiator had arrived with the SWAT. When they come, we are no longer needed because it's a hostage situation and that is their area of expertise.

Cooley and I got back in the car as Jackson got in his car. I sat there quietly as we drove to the hospital to check on Bell. About ten minutes later, we pulled into Lackey Memorial

Hospital's ER. They were in the process of seeing Bell when we came. Five minutes later, his wife came. She saw me and turned her nose up. I didn't care how she felt. That is my co-worker, and I'm just as concerned about him as everyone. Cooley spoke to his sister for a few minutes and she went in the back to see him.

We left when she came out and said, "He will be alright. The bullet scraped him."

I was glad to hear that. Cooley placed his hand on my arm with ease. He stared at me and spoke, "Let's go. I've talked to Captain, and she thinks you need to go on home."

"I have about two hours before my shift is over anyway."

"She thinks you need to go home and so do I."

CHAPTER 14

He took me back to the station and Renee asked how Bell was doing. I told her he'll be ok and how the bullet scraped him. She was happy to hear that as she went back in her area.

I clocked out and Cooley said, "I still want to come by and check on you."

"Thank you."

Going out the door, I got in my truck and left for home. All day, I couldn't think about anything, but how I did Cooley. It bothered me to know he still acted sociable to me after the way I did him. It hit me that the young girl killed herself because her boyfriend cheated on her. It never dawned on me how people take things until tonight. The girl had such much in front of her and to know she killed herself because of a boy saddened me. He will more than likely have another girl and forget about the impact he has caused someone's family forever.

Whoever Yu-Ti is, I hope her parents press charges on him for contributing to her death, but who knows; sometimes closure is closure. Unlocking the door and locking it back, I reset the alarm. I couldn't walk any further as I sat at my kitchen table and stared into the dark living room. I didn't go strip as I normally did. For some reason, my body would not let me move; my brain kept replaying the events.

The look on the girl's face was that of a lost soul, who didn't know how to get the love she deserved. Nothing had prepared me for the events that transpired from this work. I had left going to work with joy and now I returned, burdened down, sad and full of confusion. Making up my mind to get up, I took off my clothes and went straight to bed. In and out of sleep, my mind rambled. I couldn't get comfortable for the world and the world continued to sit on me. After tossing and turning for hours, I got up and sat beside the bed.

For some reason, unknown to me, I began to cry. I cried like I just heard about my dad being killed in the line of duty. I couldn't stop the tears and as funny as it seemed, I didn't want to stop crying. I finally laid back down and cried myself to sleep. Before I knew it, the day had passed and I felt better. I saw my mom had called. Not really in the mood for her, I decided to get back with her later. Then I thought about my cousin. I dialed her up. When she said hello and I didn't respond right back, she probably knew something was off.

I finally found my voice when I said, "What you doing?"

"Nothing right now. On my way to the Highway 21 Store off Old Jackson. What you need?"

"I need you to come by my crib on your way home."

"When?"

"Now if you can."

"Yeah, I can swing by before I go 10-8."

"You on duty today?"

"Yeah, we shorthanded on the jail side."

"It can wait."

"Hell, no. You my best friend and anytime you need me, I come. I don't give a damn what's going on in my life. You have my back, and I have yours."

"Well, come on."

"Bet."

"Bet."

Going into full action, I put on my blue pajama set and socks. I must get my thought process together. Taking a deep sigh, I don't have a clue how to tell her this. I don't know what she might say or anything, but I will get to the bottom of this. Some part of me doesn't want to approach her, but how can you not want to know if your best friend is fucking your ex-friend? The man you thought you'd given your heart to.

There is no way around it and I must ask her, even if in the back of my mind I know whatever she says may hurt me. Beast started barking, so I got up and saw that she was outside. I opened the door screaming, "Beast, stand down!"

Beast, as always, went in his stance for her to get out the car. She came in and gave me an "I love you" hug. I locked the door behind her. Waiting on her, she asked in her usual tone, "I heard about what happened while you were in the field, you ok?"

"I am, but it shook me up and that's for real. It made me have a strange view on family and life in general. It made me think how you could trust people and they'll throw it down the drain, just because they were being selfish."

"I believe you, because something like that can mess up the average man's mind."

My character must have given way to something more. She had an appealing innocence that was almost chaste. I waited for a few more minutes before she came out to say, "What is it, Cat? You seem like you are bothered by something."

When she asked me that, I was lost for words. She saw that I was having a tough time, she repeated, "Cat what is wrong? Is it Cooley or ya mom? What? What's wrong?"

My heart escalated to an all-time record high as it hurried blood throughout my entire body. My eyes were watering, and my ears really didn't want to receive what she had to say, but I did have to ask her. Swallowing hard, I asked in a low way that even saying it out loud felt wrong to my lips.

213

Gathering my senses, my words tumbled out. "The word came to me that you are fucking Ve-Lo and his boys for heroin, is it true?"

For a minute, I thought her lungs had a hole in it as she was there looking helpless, blowing out small puffs of air. I asked her again, "Is it true you went behind me and not only that, but you fucking Ve-Lo for some damn heroin?"

Not a word was heard from her. Tears now flooded me. As I raced up on her to almost scream in her face, I didn't know what my actions would be. I charged her with authority when I said, "Open your mouth you crack-headed bitch and tell me it isn't so! Tell me you not fucking the one man that broke my heart. You of all people know it took me a long time to finally get over him, and now I'm hearing you getting the same dick I loved. Please tell me, it's a damn lie."

Snot bubbles formed out her nose as tears flowed down her cheeks. With a broken spirit, she mumbled, "Cat."

My body literally shook from the anger within. In parts, I hoped Texan had lied but I know with something of this magnitude; it's not likely. However, I continued to look down at my best friend. I would've given my life for her, even lied for her. But now I'm blown completely away with her treachery. It took every inch of me to move away from her because if I didn't, I would use my lethal pressure points to kill her.

Backing up, I plopped in my chair as the tears had their way. I sobbed uncontrollably. I know he and I are not together, but going behind your dearest friend is something you don't do. Every emotion known to man swept through me. I had never felt so much hate as I did right then for anyone until now. As much as I loved her, I wanted to physically kill her. She knew what she did hurt me. Never in my life had it ever occurred to me that she would do me like this.

From a tone above a whisper, I heard her mention, "I never meant to do it. If I hadn't gotten caught stealing from work, I would not have gone that route. The rookie cop saw me, and I played it off. I don't think he bought it, but so far, he hadn't said a word, and I hadn't heard a word."

Half of me didn't want to hear what she was saying, but I made myself listen. I had to let her know just how big of a danger her life is in. Drying my eyes as much as I could, I stared at her with evil intentions. She couldn't look at me. I spoke with a tone that scared even me. "Look at me."

Not knowing what to think, she tilted her head towards me as I asked, "Give me one reason why I shouldn't beat the hair off your head? I mean, make it a good one, because I'm not too much into caring at the moment."

My best friend in the world started crying like she lost her best friend and technically, she might have. At this point, I'm feeling unresponsive and uncaring about her reasons. She stared up at me in such a way, that I sensed she was about to tell the truth.

"I don't know of any good reason to stop you from hurting me. If you must do it, I ask you to forgive me for what I have done to you. Our bond means the world to me and to know what I have done grieves me to my heart."

I sat there hoping this evil sensation would leave me, because I'm not myself right now and I don't know who I'm becoming, ever since I heard the shocking news. Glancing my eyes her way, she claimed, "I was in need for a new high and heard heroin was a better drug than 'caine."

I gave her a funny look and said, "You really want me to believe you think heroin is a better drug than 'caine?"

She sat up some as she retorted, "Cat, at the time that is what I thought."

"There is no excuse for what you've done; we both know it, so be honest."

"You are right and if I could take it back, I would."

"No, you wouldn't because we both know when people are strung out; they will sell their children to get whatever they need."

She was quiet as silent tears fell from her lying eyes to touch her mouth. I questioned her as nicely as I could, not really wanting to hear her answer, "How long has this been going on?"

"Which this?"

"You and Ve-Lo."

Jarissa didn't look at me. She said, "Three to four times a week for the last four months, Cat."

"Three to four times a week for the last four months?"

She tried to defend her answer by responding, "Your body doesn't crave drugs like mine. You don't know how it feels to be a slave to something and be powerless to do anything about it. You don't know the pain of wanting it so bad that you will do anything and anybody just to get the fix you need. I can!"

It still didn't register what she was going through, because she wants me to feel sorry for her and part of me wants to, but I can't. Why should I feel sorry for her when she betrayed me and our sisterhood? With tears slowing down, I wiped my eyes and asked, "You always knew drugs were a problem. What makes now any different?"

"Cat, you must believe me. I have a problem, and I need help; that is why my kids stay at Renee's. I got to the point where I put my needs ahead of theirs. I was doing things I

217

shouldn't like pawning my stuff in my crib, selling the little stamps I got. I was going downhill fast and to be honest, I saw it. I just couldn't stop it. I didn't wake up one morning and want to be a drug addict. It started with one drug, and it went from there."

"How did it get started with Ve-Lo?"

"I stole some heroin from the evidence room, and it was better than I ever heard. I already knew Ve-Lo sold it so I went to him wanting a hook-up, because they told me his dope is the shit. When I went there, I was a hundred dollars short."

Having a crackling voice and her life in my hands, I stated, "Go on."

"I needed it bad, and he put it on the table to taunt me. My soul literally shook from the sight of it. I asked him what he wanted. He said you. I told him I couldn't give him you. He said I had nothing he wanted. I couldn't think straight because the sight of the goods kept calling me."

I can tell it has really bothered her because she said, "So many times I wanted to tell you, but I couldn't bring myself to do it. I knew how you felt about him, and I knew how distraught you would be if you knew. You believe me. I never wanted to hurt you or wanted you to find out, but it happened, and I can't change it, as much as I desire to."

"Ok. Tell me all the truth now or keep all of it to yourself. Go back to the part of him saying you had nothing he wanted."

She swallowed and said, "When he said I had nothing he wanted, I told him I could give him some pussy. He said he would rather have head."

She paused and so did my caring when I asked as nicely as I could, "Did you suck or fuck?"

Sadly, she bellowed out softly, "Cat. Please don't ask me that. It's in the past."

"It isn't in the past because you are not delivered. I'm an officer and I know about drugs and the people that use them so try another answer. Did you suck or fuck?"

Jarissa was crying and not trying to answer me. In a demanding but raised tone, my words to her were, "It is in your best interest you tell me how things started between you and Ve-Lo. That is the only thing I'm concerned about. Because every time I would try and tell you about your problem, you'd shut me down and tell me how grown and in control you are. So, forget that crap you talking about and answer my fucking question. Did you suck or fuck?"

After asking her twice, I wasn't going to ask again but she replied, "Mostly head with a dab of heroin on it. But I did both."

My best friend felt my reaction as she folded her hands up to protect her face, but that didn't stop me. I jumped on her as she sat. My short arms were turning her head every which way but loose. Jumping on my best friend has never happened in all my twenty-five years. If anything, I was kicking ass for her and not kicking her ass. I didn't know I had reacted in that way until, I heard her crying and crying. She was not fighting me back as I wanted, but I didn't care.

Sadly, she told me a little too much and to know she had her mouth on my ex made me aim for hers violently. I was trying to knock every tooth she had out, but I only drew a lot of blood. I don't know how long I was hitting her, but the only way I stopped was when I heard her begging me to. At that moment, my assault on her came to a standstill. Tears rained down on me as I saw her bloody face. I had to quit because there's no fun in beating someone up, if they don't fight back, and I couldn't do it anymore.

She sat there in pain no doubt but drunk from the fight. The more I glared at her, unemotional and unfeeling, the angrier I got. I stated coldly, "I never knew I would hurt like this. You were my best friend. My only best friend and you did this to me."

"I'm sorry. I promise I am."

Still dazed and confused, I opened the door to say, "Beast, stand down."

My eyes went back over to her, and I said, "You my family, my best friend and someone I have loved, but, as of today, goodbye. I don't care if I don't ever see or speak to you again. I don't care if we ever get over this, I don't want anything to do with you. Get out my house and stay the hell out my life. The earth isn't big enough for the both of us. But, if I hear about you doing him again, you will wish for death."

My girl got up crying, bloody and trying to hug me. I pushed her off me and she stumbled out the door. She fell to her knees crying, but I was not fazed. I heard her crying with her heart while she cried out, "This isn't goodbye. Cat, please; I can't say goodbye right now."

Spitting in her direction, I slammed the door. When I heard the ignition, I locked the door and went to shower. So much crossed me as the water trickled onto my skin. I know drugs will make you do crazy stuff, but I never once imagined it to happen to me. I've seen it with my own eyes and heard it with my own ears, how drugs can drive people to do things beyond their control, but my girl was different. In truth, she wasn't different; I just made her out to be.

She wasn't like the other people I've arrested or encountered; she was my girl, point blank. My heart feels irreparable. The pain of knowing your best friend did that to you is far worse than a man breaking your heart for a woman you don't care for. I sat there for what seemed like hours before I could move. My mind still wrapped around what transpired between my girl and me. Drying my eyes, I got up to clean the blood up.

After cleaning up the blood splatters, I settled my thoughts and feelings; I went out and did drills with Beast for hours. I decided to do my own drills by punching the bag and kicking my stick man. I didn't hear anyone approach until I heard a voice, "You must be really upset about something."

I stopped and saw that it was Momma. I took off my gloves and went over to her and gave her a hug. She placed her arms about me and said, "It's alright, baby, Momma's here for you."

The anger turned to tears as I held onto my momma. Seconds later, I backed up and said, "Let's go in the house."

She went in first and the cold air felt just right after I'd worked up a good sweat.

"You want something to drink?"

"No, I'm good."

Sitting down, I almost cried again before saying, "I jumped on my best friend this morning, because I found out she was sleeping around with Ve-Lo."

"The drug dealer from the tracks?"

"Yes, the one and only."

"Weren't you crazy about him not too long ago?"

"I was."

"I'm sure she didn't mean to do it."

"But she did, and I know she knew what she was doing. I don't understand why it made me so angry to find out that she was sleeping with him."

"You were angry because he was your first everything. He broke your heart and instead of healing, you just moved on."

It made sense once I heard her say it. Using a more sincere tone, my mother spoke with care. "Cat, you need to call Jarissa or go see her; she is going to need a friend."

"Why is that, Ma? She hurt me."

"Indictment orders came down and her name is on it for stealing evidence from police property."

If I wasn't sitting, I would've fallen. She added, "The new rookie cop, the one that was giving you a challenging time, was a mole. We knew our evidence was disappearing for major drug dealers, but we didn't know how. She wasn't taking it for them but for her to use. However, that was one reason why the other investigator left. He had his hands in it, but we couldn't pin it on him, so he resigned and did another tour of duty. Nevertheless, my niece kept it up. He turned evidence on her, because he knew she had a key made. He chose to save his own rump."

"Does she know?"

"She will, come Monday morning. She will be locked up and processed like the people she has done on many occasions. She'll have to bond out, but the good thing is the dockets are backlogged, so it could be months before she has to do anything about it. Now, did you know?"

I'd never lied to my momma, and I wasn't going to start.

"I knew about the drug use and the stealing."

"Why didn't you tell me?"

"She and I talked, and she told me she buys it now, because the cop was watching."

"By then it was too late, he had already pinned for the crime. According to the time frame, she has been doing this for almost two years," Momma said.

"Two years? I didn't know she was on that stuff that long. I only knew about a year, right after my ordeal with Ve-Lo, but she never really stated how she got it."

"She's looking at evidence tampering, stealing from state property and one year per evidence item she has stolen. My niece is looking at over fifty years. Hopefully, the judge will have compassion and give her rehab with the rest of the years on paper; since she has worked for the state that could be in her favor."

"Ma, I should have said something to you about it."

"Catherine, don't you know you could get into trouble just because you knew, and you didn't report it? Your job is to uphold the law in *every* aspect, not just because we all wear a badge. You were given an oath to do a job and you failed."

"Am I in trouble?"

She was quiet before letting out, "No you are not in trouble because there is no actual proof that you knew. But, from here on out, you need to keep your nose clean. I plan to leave ASAP, and I've already made my recommendations. Cooley will be promoted to captain and you, the lead investigator. I believe you both can run headquarters and make it better than ever."

Momma left, but her words remained as I sat there, worn out with life and tired of fighting.

CHAPTER 15

Sunday morning, I got up, got dressed, turned on the alarm, locked the door and went to church. Midway in the pews, were Cooley and his son, Preston. I didn't want to sit near them, but the usher pressed me in that direction. He looked up and saw me. Not giving away his true feelings, he moved out the way to let me in on the other side of his son.

His son laid his head on my lap as he usually did whenever I went to service and Cooley didn't say a word.

The preacher stood up and said in a booming voice, "Life is a puff of smoke. No matter how you smoke it, choke it or shotgun it, your life is still a puff of smoke, Amen?"

"Amen," the congregation repeated.

"While you are on this here old earth, you must prepare for leaving this dear old earth. Some of you like to smoke your lives. You just go by day by day with your lives, not caring about your soul's salvation or anyone else's. Then, you have some that choke their lives. You try to do things, but it doesn't work, because The Lord Jesus isn't in it. By that you have problems doing what you need to do because you are not full circle; you keep stalling. Last of all, there are the ones that like to shotgun their lives. You are the ones that like things fast as a microwave and you feel all you need to do is be risky, partake in everything and think of consequences later, Amen?"

"Amen," the congregation agreed.

"Wake up, you sluggards. While you are playing with your lives, someone wishes they had theirs. While you are choking out on the things of God, somebody wants to add more gas and accelerate. While you are living dangerously, somebody wants to live, period. You should do what is important to you and I don't mean things on this earth. You as chosen vessel of The Lord and you must come full circle and forsake all others, like the disciples did. You have to consent for Christ to lead you and guide you to all truths. You can't expect a rich lifestyle being broke. You can't expect the blessings of God, shacking up with Satan. Get your mind right, because you can't do it on your own. The Lord must help you and that is only if you allow *him* to. Bow your heads as I pray: *Lamb of God, you know our hearts and you know which lifestyle we all live. I ask you this day to help us to live accordingly to your will and your word. We are not perfect, but you are a perfect God. In Jesus' name, let us all say Amen, Amen."*

The preacher asked, "Who all needs prayer?" I normally sit in my seat but today, I didn't. Cooley was stunned to see me get up. As the lady anointed my head, the preacher asked, "What can the Lord do for you?"

"I have a best friend that needs deliverance, and I need the man I love to forgive me."

"Close your eyes and believe God."

Upon closing my eyes, I cried. Tears just kept falling. The longer I stood there, the more they fell. After crying until I felt better, I left out as others were doing the same. Cooley came behind me and stopped me before I got in my truck. I was stunned to see him standing this close to me. Staring up at him, he said, "I heard what you said to the preacher."

I couldn't remove my eyes from his, because his face is the face I want to gaze upon, possibly for the rest of my life. He got a little closer to my face as he spoke. "Am I the man you love?"

"Cooley, I love you and I didn't realize it until the day I snapped on you."

"Catherine, I love you and to hear you say that means so much to me."

"It feels good to hear me say that."

"What you doing tonight?"

"I'll be home."

"May I come by?"

"I wouldn't have it any other way."

I got in the car and left. When I got home, I didn't open the gate. O.B. was there. I'm really not feeling him, but I do need someone to talk to. Getting out my truck, I stood at his window. He rolled it down.

"What are you doing here?"

"I came to check on you and I miss you."

"What you miss? Making me choose between what I want and saving your woman?"

"I never should have said that I'm sorry. You can say I was desperate and all into you."

I didn't say a word. He asked, "May I come in?"

"Only for a few."

I opened the gate and got in my truck. Soon as I parked, Beast was barking.

"Let me feed him."

O.B. stood by and watched me feed Beast. I let Beast go and he roamed the yard happily. Upon unlocking the door, I turned off the alarm and locked the door behind me. O.B. went in the living room as I went to change. When I made it back to the living room, he was sitting on the couch. I sat in the chair and talked.

No funny business occurred. We talked like old times. He made me remember why I started messing with him in the first place. It is for his sense of humor; his good looks and the way we have chemistry. He and I laughed as tension build up. I was not going to make that mistake and sleep with O.B. because of my new existing love for Cooley. O.B. stated, "Cat, you will always have a part of me and you can't change that, no matter what you try. All I ask is you allow me to be with you one last time."

I fidgeted in my seat as my lower parts screamed, *yes*. He licked his lips and whispered, "I want to taste you and kiss your pussy lips long as you'll let me."

My flesh took over and I was soon letting O.B. have his way with me. Soon as he was finished, I was ashamed and knew it was wrong. I never should have agreed to let him come in because I know how weak I could be around him. But he did tell me he wouldn't do anything else to me I don't want him to. I believed him and before he left, he said he will always be there for me. Soon as he left, I put Beast up, took a shower and waited for Cooley. It was seven o'clock and he was still a no-show. By ten, I called it the night. Soon as I got in the bed, he knocked on the door. I jumped out the bed because I knew it was him.

Opening the door, I saw that it was indeed him. He said, "Sorry, my sister and Bell were arguing, and she kicked him out."

"Come on in," I replied as he came in and I locked the door. Cooley placed his arms around me and stared into my face.

There is something about being in his arms like this felt so right to me. I knew he was searching my face for any trace of anything. I was not going to let on that I just been with an old friend. Placing my head as close to his chest as I could, I inhaled his scent. Now I see how you can love someone and do what you do. It made me feel like a liar and a cheat. Cooley doesn't deserve the way I have been unfaithful to him or his love. He said, "Cat, I need you to love me with your whole heart and don't lie. I need to know you are down with me and you won't turn your back on me."

"Cooley, there are some things I must come full circle with first."

"Ok, what?"

Those words didn't leave my mouth good before he got a call, stating that Bell was back at his sister's house acting a fool. I hate we didn't finish our conversation before he rushed off. I wanted to call Bell and see what was going on, but I already had the idea. I called Renee and told her about the fight. She couldn't believe it and just by hearing it, neither could I. When I mentioned Jarissa will be indicted tomorrow, she cried.

Ever since I came on the scene, the three of us have been the girls in blue, with different personalities. Renee would always be the one that gave sound advice. Jarissa is always the one who starts trouble or is in some trouble, while I'm always the one who fights and doesn't care. Together, we were a perfect fit but now, it seems like we are falling apart. Renee said she was going to call her sister and talk to her. I want to talk to her, but don't know if I'm completely ready to see her or hear her voice. She's still my girl; right now, she is just a little further back from me. Renee wants me to talk to her, but I don't want to. I hung up with Renee, checked on Preston and went to bed.

Around four am, I got a phone call. I was sound asleep but picked up anyway.

"Hello."

"Cat."

My eyes flew open. It was Jarissa.

"Hello, Cat, you there?"

"Yeah, what do you want?"

"I know you know I got indicted."

"I do."

"I'm not coming to work. They gonna have to give it to me at home and not in front of people I know."

"And you called me, why?"

232

"To ask for your forgiveness again and to let you know I love you."

Deciding to sit up in the bed, while the thunder played in the sky, I didn't answer her. She must have assumed that I didn't hear her, because she asked, "Cat, you hear me?"

"Yeah, I do. Just because I forgive you, don't mean I have to talk to you."

"Having your forgiveness means so much to me and if you don't want to talk to me, that's fine. I can live with that and now I can sleep."

She got off the phone and now I'm awake. It was odd for her to call me, but I'm somewhat relieved we talked. Taking a deep sigh, I went back to bed and this time, I thought about my future and leaving the Scott County Police Department. Our day-to-day routine was different, but quieter. Everyone was moving up the chain of command and new people were coming on the shift. It wasn't the same. Our jesting was at a minimum because every night in the county, the people were acting up and sometimes, we let some go because of the overcrowding.

I take it that it's because the weather has warmed up and so has crimes. Sometimes, we all didn't have time to speak because of all the 10-47's. The disturbances were frequent and too many. All the people at headquarters stayed busy. Since she's not working, the place is boring and odd. Though, letting up was nowhere in sight as the job became more demanding. For the first time, I'm not being a bad ass, and my language is appropriate.

In a few months, my mom will be retiring and making Cooley my boss. We already knew the rules about fraternizing, so we're very careful not to be seen together, and for the most part, we kept it professional. I had put in my transfer to the Morton K-9 Unit and was waiting on the opening. They say it would be within another month, but I can't wait. Preston was calling me Momma Cat and I loved that little boy as if he were my own.

I understand now, when Cooley used to talk about being a role model and doing your best for your child. This little boy means so much to me and then some. As for me and O.B., I let it go and we're only friends. Occasionally, I would see him staring at me and doing moving his mouth silently, so I'll know what he is thinking. Jackson is in line to be an investigator, because I'm awaiting a transfer. Meanwhile, Bell wanted to stay a regular cop; in addition, he and his wife were doing better since he moved back home.

Everything was great, life was good. Renee was on maternity leave and Jarissa was awaiting trial. Today when I got off from work, she called me. We talked and talked like nothing happened, although, she and I don't hang out like we used to. We are still family and if she needed anything, I would still do it for her, and she knows it. Just because we didn't do what we used to, didn't mean anything. She had her own things going on and so did I. Her thing included doing her and when I didn't talk to her, I was thankful that Renee keeps me informed.

From my understanding, she hired a lawyer and has her children. Renee says Jarissa's has been clean and getting herself together to make it look good in front of the judge. I had told Renee to let Jarissa know I'm so proud of her and I know she can beat this thing and kick the habit. Later Renee told me Jarissa was happy to know I was proud of her and for the most part, it gave me a good feeling. When I got off from work that morning, I turned off the alarm and locked the door.

Strangely enough, I debated about seeing my girl in court. I told Renee to tell her I may come but it solely depended on the time. The word got back to me she couldn't wait to see me. I was feeling hopeful and not letting what happened between us, get to me. Once my shower ended, I got in the bed. For the life of me, I couldn't sleep. I got up and closed the curtains, to ensure no light could get in. Soon as I laid down, my cell started ringing.

I ignored it and turned over to place a pillow on my head. My cell began to ring back-to-back. Becoming agitated, I jumped up, snatched the phone and screamed, "Who the hell is this!"

The caller was screaming and carrying on. I removed the phone from my ear and saw it was Renee. Placing the phone back to my ear, I stated, "Calm down. I can't hear you."

She tried to muffle her cry, but she wasn't doing a good job. As if her voice cleared away like the clouds of a storm, she said, "Jarissa's dead."

Not believing I heard it right, my heart raced as I asked, "Who is dead?"

Through all the screaming, I heard, "Jarissa."

To hear she's gone makes me believe it's a mistake. I thought, maybe I heard it wrong, so I asked again, "You said Jarissa is dead?"

"Oh, Cat; she's gone. She's gone! I found her on my way to work. She told me last night to come by and see her before I go to work. Please, God, help me."

Renee was crying hard, and her words were not understandable. How can you be prepared to hear your best friend is gone? How can you picture your life without them on earth? You can't. You know, best friends fuss, fight and quit speaking, but just like family; you all start back as if nothing happened. Not caring about anything other than getting to her, I couldn't remember flying through Hillsboro to get to Lone Pilgrim. I risked my own life just to get to her.

When I got there, the coroner was there pronouncing her dead. I shuddered at the sight. Everyone in the neighborhood was standing about as the early morning day shift was working the scene. They saw me and held me back. They knew she was family and knew I would try to see what happened. Renee was acting up more than I was. My mom was there, and she was crying just as hard as the both of us. The rookie cop was there and I went for him, because if he had not reported her, she would still be alive today. Because he was after brownie points, my best friend was now dead.

He stated to me, "Settle down, Officer Le Beau. I know you're hurt, but you can't blame anyone."

"Fuck you!" I screamed at him.

Momma came to me and held me. The rookie cop left as he continued to do his job. I couldn't understand it. She was doing so well. She was clean and had her children back. Her outlook on her crime was in her favor, because Momma made a few calls on her behalf. Renee was just crying, but I needed answers. Somebody had to tell me something. A day shift officer said, "Cat, calm down. It isn't that officer's fault."

"How can you say that? He was the one to turn her in!" I yelled.

Momma said, "Girls, listen to me. Jarissa overdosed on heroin."

"How is that possible, when she was clean?" Cat asked.

"She hid it so well," Momma replied.

"Momma, I can't believe it, oh God; I can't believe it. Please tell me I'm dreaming."

"Cat, go home and go to sleep. You too, Renee. Neither of you can do anything here. Right now, you have to get out the way and let these great men do their duties."

"Where are her children?" Cat asked.

"They are at their grandparents' and I'm on my way to get them." Renee said.

"Okay," Momma said.

"If I can't blame the rookie, then how about the one that sold it to her?"

"Cat, let it go, because right now you are fishing for fish in a huge pond. No one will own up to selling her anything. Go home and get some rest."

Momma tried pulling me away, but it was a hard process. I was being my usual stubborn self. I didn't want to leave her house. My best friend is gone, and I still can't believe it. *There is no way she killed herself.* Someone that had it all would not end it suddenly with a needle in their arm. I spoke loud enough for all to hear, "I'm going to get whoever did this to her."

"Catherine, you can't be a vigilante. Let the system work. But trust me; I've worked my share of cases like this."

"Jarissa isn't a damn case. She's family and I know she didn't do this to herself."

My mother snatched me around and spoke loudly, "Catherine, listen to yourself. Think about how others feel when we as officers, tag and bag their loved ones. To us it is a case, but they feel as you are feeling right now. I have worked cases after cases like this and I know from what I have seen, she did this to herself. It's a harsh fact, but a fact nonetheless."

I jerked away from her, and she grabbed me again. This time I didn't. She pulled me to her and told me it's going to be ok. I know my mother knows best and right now; I need to believe what she is saying is of a truth. When the funeral home came and got the body. I just stood there and watched. They had her covered up as they put her in the back. Once the body left, the crowd dissipated slowly. I couldn't move, even Momma and Renee had left.

I knew what Momma said, but I still had to ask. Going to my car, I dialed him up. The first thing he said was, "Sorry about ya girl."

Not caring what came out his mouth, I asked with a definitive, cut-throat attitude, "Did you sell those drugs to her, Ve-Lo?"

"No. She quit getting it from me. I told her yesterday to go back and get her drugs from the one supplier she been going to. I told her I don't know about the others, but I know mine is a trusted batch and she would do better with mine, but she declined."

"Did she decline before or after she quit fucking you?"

He started laughing and announced, "What is it to you?"

"You one dirty-ass bastard."

"A dirty bastard you loved."

"Yeah, you said it right; *loved*. And if you hadn't done what you did; I might not have been where I am today. For that, I say thank you. I just want to know. Do you know who sold it to her?"

"No. You the top-notch detective, figure it out."

I hung up on him and drove home. I didn't feel like getting out the truck, so I sat there. I looked at my phone. So many things I wished I'd said to her but hadn't. Getting out the truck, I gave Beast a lot of food and water. To make sure I had no company, Beast was left to roam the perimeter. Just watching him and wishing Jarissa was here, with a defeated

240

spirit, I went in the house, turned off the alarm and locked the door.

Not having the desire to do anything, I texted Cooley and told him I wasn't coming in and I didn't know when I would return. I didn't wait for his reply, and I didn't care what his reply was. If he wanted to fire me, let him do so. I lost my best friend, and I still can't believe it. Stripping off, I took some sleeping pills and went to bed.

CHAPTER 16

I must have slept for almost two days. When I awoke this evening, I had over fifty missed calls and too many texts. I woke up and remembered Jarissa was one. I laid there staring at the ceiling, lost in thought. My every thought was of my best friend and how she is no longer walking on the earth. Feeding Beast didn't cross my mind, and living didn't cross my mind. Finding the strength to get up took a toll on me. Every time I wanted to get up, I wouldn't. I would lay in the bed and just sleep. I didn't want to hear anything else or talk to anyone, especially if they didn't have any news about Jarissa. I prayed that maybe I was being pranked on an ultimate level.

My mom called and I wouldn't talk to her either. She knows I'm depressed and just want to be alone. I've always been this way. If something bothered me, I would shut everyone out until the stink passed. Sometimes it would pass faster than other times, but this was something I wasn't sure I was ready to just let go. Turning over, I saw Renee calling. I didn't answer the phone for her either. I feel incomplete and totally lost. It's one thing to be mad at her and able to see her but to be mad at her and never to see her again is unbearable.

My cell phone rang again, and I turned the ringer off. I left a voicemail stating to everyone who'd call that I'm ok and just want to be left alone. Taking a few more pm pills, I cried myself back to sleep. I don't know how long I was out, but knocking disturbed my sleep. I got up and fell to the floor by my night table. I hadn't walked or gone to the bathroom in so long, my legs were asleep. Suddenly, I heard a loud kick. Having no idea who it was, I snatched my nine off the night table and lay back against the wall. I was prepared for whoever it was. Louder than ever, I heard, "Don't shoot! Don't shoot! It's me, O.B."

Lowering my personal gun, I sat there on the floor. He picked me up and helped me stand to my feet. My legs gave out again, which caused me to fall into his arms. O.B. placed me on my bed. He came at me, saying, "Sorry about your door, but I had to come see you."

"How did you get by Beast?"

"He was around back when I broke in."

My head spun away from him. He said, "I have been worried sick about you."

"If you called my phone, you would've heard my voicemail message to everyone that calls me, which, I checked."

"I heard it go to voicemail, I just had to see you anyway. Let me put your door up first then I'll come back in here."

"Help me up. I will go with you and sit in the living room. Been lying in this bed for days anyway; it's time for me to get up."

O.B. helped me off the bed and guided me up the hall to the living room. I sat in my usual seat. This time, I glanced around and saw my door. "You know you going to pay for that, right?"

I watched him put my door back on the hinges. They were loose, but my door still locked, even though it didn't look like it did at first. In case he didn't hear what, I said, I said it again, "You know you going to pay for that, right?"

"I heard you, Cat, but it doesn't matter. I thought you were..."

"Were what?"

His voice became weak and inaudible, "I don't know..."

O.B. got on his knees in front of me and held my hands tenderly. Taking his time, he lifted my hands to his lips and kissed them sweetly as he stated sorrowfully, "I was afraid you might have done something stupid, or pissed off the wrong person about Jarissa and they might have done something stupid to you. If the second one was true, I wasn't leaving any rock unturned until I found out what happened."

"For me?"

"Anything for you, Cat. You have been my dearest friend and at one point, my lover."

That gave me a small smile. He lifted my head towards his. He said, "Cat, we all loved your cousin, with 'her knowing everything' ass, but God loved her best. We must accept what has happened and deal with it the best we can."

"I don't want to deal with it. I don't want to let her go."

"Cat, you must. You will need closure like Renee."

"She was my best friend, and a piece of old dick broke that up."

"Everything happens for a reason."

"I don't like the reasons. I just want her back."

"Cat, there is nothing we can do to bring her back. Absolutely nothing we can ever attempt to put life back in her."

"I know, I guess I'm in denial."

"You hungry? I can get you something to eat or fix you a sandwich."

"I'm not hungry."

"But you have to eat. You still need your strength. You still have to live, even if you don't want to."

I didn't answer as O.B. got up and fixed me a sandwich in the kitchen. I didn't want it, but I forced myself to eat it. I didn't care to eat and wanted to throw the food under the couch or something, but he would not let me out his sight. He saw me looking around and he told me to my face, "You might as well eat up, because I'm not getting up until you do."

"What makes you think that? You are not my husband."

"No, I'm not, but I knew you long before I got married."

I finished the food and as he took the plate to the kitchen, I checked my messages and heard what Renee said. When he sat back down, I said, "I got Renee's message that we view the body day after tomorrow."

"You up to that?"

"No, not really."

"Maybe if you see her, it will make you feel better."

"Maybe?"

"Did she say anything about the funeral?"

"It's Saturday at two."

"I don't know if I will be able or ready to see her."

"If you need me to be by your side, I will. We have been best buds for a long time and right now, you need a friend."

"How is it you seem to know what I need?"

"When you care so much for someone, what they need is automatically hooked up to yours."

"Really?"

"Yes."

We were quiet as O.B. continued to stay on his knees in front of me. Sex nor anything erotic crossed my mind. Right now, he was being my friend and that is what I needed more than anything. He got up and said, "I know what we can do."

"What can we do?"

"We can talk about Jarissa."

I looked at him crossways to ask, "Why?"

"It's a type of therapy that will help you cope with your feelings. We can talk about the times you spent with her. You will always have those memories. I've learned talking about people you love helps."

"Really?"

"Once you talk about her, talk about your love for Cooley."

At the mention of his name, O.B.'s persona went dim. I know it hurts him for me to discuss Cooley, but it's not about him. I need to talk to someone, and he has been nothing more than a friend. O.B. got off his knees and sat beside me.

Tilting my head towards his, I cried softly as I stated, "I'm so damn tired of crying."

"It be like that sometimes. But you a fighter and I don't think ya girl would want you moping around."

"I don't think she would either, but I can't help it right now. What all is the outside world saying?"

"It's hard to believe she's gone and how headquarters isn't the same."

"Everything has just changed."

"Renee said she got a letter from Jarissa," O.B. spoke as if it was a normal occurrence.

"What letter?"

"I don't know. She said she just got a letter from Jarissa," he said as if I knew.

"How is that possible?"

"She mailed it off before she died. You need to check and see if you got one. When was the last time you checked your mail anyway?" O.B. added.

"It's been a few days."

"Go check it. I will walk with you," O.B. spoke as we got up and walked to the mailbox. The light hurt my eyes some and it made me hold my head back some.

"It's just the sun, vampire."

That made me smile a little as we walked to the mailbox. I didn't have a letter. I closed the mailbox lid back and faced him. "O.B., you know what?"

"What?"

"I'm going to go to work."

"Since you up to it; why not? Getting back in the swing could do you justice," he spoke with a little confidence.

He walked me up to my door and said, "If it helps, I'm sorry this happened. If you need anything, I'm here for you."

I gave him a hug and he left. I locked the door and went to shower. An optimistic feeling overcame me. I feel better, not one hundred percent, but better. After I got dressed, I turned on the alarm and locked the door. Going to my truck, I decided to take Beast. He was happy and that made me somewhat happy.

After about ten minutes of riding, I did feel better. When I arrived at the station, I placed Beast in the dog area. Everyone was surprised to see me. Jackson spoke first. "If it isn't the living dead."

"Yeah, yeah, yeah."

While hugging me, my devoted friend murmured, "Good to see you, girl," as he gave me a hearty hug and squeeze.

I felt happy as I responded, "Jackson, it is good to be back."

As I absorbed the laughter I've missed and the smiling faces I needed, Jackson stated with much joy, "Just because you back, don't mean you have to kick ass as fast."

"If they don't want any, they better not bring any."

"Catherine, come in my office." I looked and saw it was Captain Cooley.

Jackson, being the usual comedian he normally is, quipped, "Dang, Wild Cat. You just got back and already you in the office. What you do on your day off for that?"

They all laughed when I clapped back, "You couldn't make it at the firing range, so he wants me to take your place."

We all laughed as I walked off towards the door. I knocked and he told me to come in. I stood there. He got up and gave me a squeeze. It was amazing to be in his arms like this. Captain Cooley said kindly, "Sit down."

He went back to his seat, and I sat across from him. I just got back, and I don't know what could be wrong. I asked, clueless, "What is it?"

"I want to tell you that I'm sorry for your loss. I know she was your best friend through all the things you both had been through."

"Thank you, Captain Cooley."

"You know you can take time off."

"I don't need it."

"Catherine, your safety and the safety of your fellow officers is important. I believe they can provide for this department in your absence. I don't want you to be here half-cocked and not thinking clearly. You can get hurt, if not killed, in these streets. I still love you and I want what is best for you."

"Cooley. I mean Captain Cooley; I didn't mean to—"

He cut me off as he stated, "It's ok."

"No, it's not ok. I didn't mean to."

"Catherine, it's ok. I don't want to talk about how you did me. We can discuss that later. Right now, I need to know you are up to doing your duty to the best of your ability."

"Let me try. If I don't feel it, I can do it, I will let you know."

"That'll be fine. You have almost seven hundred and fifty hours you can take with pay. That's a little over two months."

"I'm good. Just need to be here to get her off my mind."

"I have to go out of town and should make it back the day of the funeral. If I do, I would love to escort you."

"I would like that, Captain Cooley."

"You can go back out there where all the jokes are," he said with a smile.

I left the office. Bell and Jackson were still there, sitting at their desks, pretending to work. Having my usual smile, I blared, "You guys don't have anything else to do but sit down to make your money? I mean, the streets need detail, not desk duty."

"We earn ours, believe that" Bell said.

"Jackson, you riding with Bell this week?"

"Yeah, because my car needs some work on it."

251

"You mean you were supposed to be my partner as investigators, but you would rather work the field with Bell until then?"

Shaking his head as if he couldn't decide, he laughed as he spoke, "Yeah."

"Guess, I'll patrol too."

They left me as I sat at my desk for a few moments. It hit me Jarissa isn't going to walk through our connecting halls, just to see what is going on, from the county side of the department. She isn't going to come over and I wasn't going to go over there to tell the latest gossip. I heard a voice asking, "Cat, you, ok?"

"Yeah, about to drive out to Hawkins Road; you know Over-In-The-Woods community."

"Okay."

I got up and left out the door. Taking Beast out the dog area, we got in my old patrol car and left towards the country. He was in the back with the window and barking. It felt like the good old days, before Cooley came and O.B. came back into my life. No sooner than I'd almost turned onto Hawkins Road, a car passed me and turned up a beer. Quickly, I turned on my lights and they pulled over. I walked slowly to the car and saw it was crazy Chipmunk. He rocked his head a little and slurred his words. "Hey, crazy. What you doing out here?"

"Working. What you doing out here?"

"I have a cold and went to get some medicine, then I stopped by my grandson's house."

"It's obvious that you are drunk. You can call someone to come get you and the car, or I take you to jail, and the car gets towed?"

"I take my chances to call."

"Hurry up."

I stood there and watched him. He could barely use the phone. I took the phone and told his sister what was happening. She came and got the car and her brother. When they left, I let Beast out and he ran around for a few as he pissed on the ground. I commanded, "Beast, in."

Beast came to my call, and we left. On my way, I saw Jackson and Bell conducting a roadblock at the intersection of Ringo Road and Old Jackson Road. I pulled my car over and went over to them. Bell said, as he let the car go through, "Don't come here making us chase a car tonight."

"Do your job, or do I have to show you how to do it?"

"That's a good one," Jackson added.

"I was on my way in and saw the county boys needed some help."

"Help yourself on to the station," Jackson said as he handed the lady back her license.

"Cool. It looks like rain, and I don't want to get caught in it."

"We're about to quit anyway."

I left and made it back to the station. I really didn't want to be at work. I called Cooley and told him, and he was ok with it. I took Beast out, parked the car and clocked out and went home.

CHAPTER 17

I woke up and didn't want to get up. Today is the day we are to view the body. I called Momma and told her I couldn't do it. She understood. Renee called me and told me she wanted me there. I told her I couldn't do it, and she believed me, because Jarissa was more like my sister than hers. After feeding Beast, I took a pm pill and went back to sleep. All I want to do is sleep until the funeral. I don't want to socialize or talk to anyone about her.

As time crept without my consent, I got up and saw Momma pull up. She got out her truck and walked right in. Her first question was, "How you doing?"

"I'm just doing."

"I just came from seeing the body at Holifield."

"And?"

"And she looks like she is just sleeping."

We both were quiet before she asked, "You going to be ok for tomorrow?"

"Yes."

"Cooley coming?" Momma asked.

"He will, if he's back in time for the funeral."

"Renee and I want you to ride with us in the Suburban."

"What about the kids?"

"They will be riding with us. We all are her only close family."

"I know."

"That is why family time is a valuable time. We don't know when it is our turn to leave this shell of a body behind."

My words wouldn't come; my mouth opened, but nothing came out. Momma felt I wasn't into talking as she replied, "I have to go. You are to come over sometime. We love you and miss you."

"I will, but with all this going on, I won't be much company."

"I understand."

She gave me a hug and left, and I went back to sleep. All during the night, I tossed and turned. Nothing I did worked to stop me from thinking about what's about to happen in hours. My eyes glanced at the clock, every hour on the hour. I couldn't get comfortable, and I couldn't go to sleep for the world. Finally, at two am, I took a sleeping pill and went to sleep. I awoke to a pleasant day. The sun was out but hid back and forth behind clouds.

Looking in the mirror, I saw a scared young woman, afraid of what today is going to bring. Deciding not to wear my uniform, I wore in its place a three-piece, long black skirt set. I allowed my hair to hang as I placed on my best-friend necklace; I had gotten from her that Christmas. Stepdad Stuart pulled up with everyone in the car. I spoke as I got in. We took off towards Holifield Funeral Home in Forest to follow the body. Renee said, "Cat, in my letter, she asked for a song to play. We can talk about it later."

I didn't ask, because I didn't know how strong of a voice I would have. I continued to stare out the window. Soon as we arrived, the place was already packed. There were so many people there to follow the body. Never had I seen so many cop cars, since my dad's funeral. It brought tears to my eyes to see so many people coming out to show their love for her and support for us. In uniform, I saw Jackson and Bell on the other side of the building, along with the other Scott County boys; however, I didn't see Cooley.

We sat there as the directors were lining us up. Moments later, the car came out with the body. I closed my eyes. I didn't want to see it just yet. Renee saw me and said in a small, still tone, "Cat, you're going to have to see it."

"I know."

With our lights on, we pulled out and began the longest journey towards Sebastopol. For the duration of the trip up Highway 21, I thought about all the things she and I had done and been through. Everything came to mind as I saw my scenery change. I have done so much with her, and we talked all the time. Now she is gone and I'm alone.

Upon arriving at the school, cars were already there. I was beginning to think that our home school was going to be too small. The parking attendants guided everyone to parking places. Soon as we parked, I got out with my heart and my nerves on my sleeve. The directors began to put us in order. I had my head straight forward as I felt a hand upon mine. I jumped some and saw it was O.B.

With a surprised tone, I asked, "O.B. what are you doing?"

"I'm not letting you go through this alone. She was my friend, and I love you. So, I don't care who sees me with you. I need to be with you in your time of sorrow and if she doesn't understand, she can leave."

When they pulled the coffin out on the roller, I froze. It was the exact coffin we talked about when we were filling out paperwork for our burial insurance. She described my coffin, and I did hers. Here it is now in my face, a baby blue coffin with white trimmings. Now, I'm nervous, because there is an inscription at the opener, and I won't know until they open it up. I grabbed O.B.'s arm and leaned into him. We began walking through the lower door of the gym. Then out of nowhere, I heard the song "Bye-Bye," by Mariah Carey. A few years ago, she sang that song for me. I took it as a joke because we were clowning and drunk. That is the song she said she wanted to play for me. It would be a reminder of all the good and bad times we had, and how she would be telling me her final goodbye.

I told her I would leave this world before her because of my line of duty, but she said she would, because that's how it always ends up being. So far, she was right. I'm here to bury her and not the other way around. I didn't think I could walk as I heard that song play. The preacher's saying their scripture walk didn't fade me. My ears could only here her saying, "Bye-Bye." I could only see her singing the song to me and not my surroundings. The entire song brought back everything I had been avoiding. I didn't want to feel, I didn't want to know about anything anymore, because my best friend was gone.

O.B. must have heard me moaning in my cries, because he grabbed onto me harder, as if to say, "I'm here, Cat."

I didn't think I was going to make it if he wasn't holding me up. I spoke softly to decree; while sitting a few feet away from the coffin, "No God, no. My best friend. God, no. Not my best friend."

When everyone sat in their chairs, I saw one area for cops, and it was jam-packed with everyone that knew her; even her classmates where there as they all had napkins in their

259

hands. My girl was truly loved by many people in our small town and today they are showing it. I sat there with O.B. at my side motionless. My mind was not comprehending the loss of her and nor was it understanding anything else. No matter how I tried to listen to the order of service, I kept my eyes on her coffin; in part I hoped she was not there and hoped it was all a lie.

Once the preacher put the service back in the hands of the directors, I literally wanted to stop breathing. They opened the coffin and there she was. From this view, she looked the same. They began to play "Bye-Bye" again. People were going by and crying as they came away from the coffin. My momma and Stepdad Stuart stood there for a few minutes before Momma began to cry hysterically. Jarissa and Renee are her sister's only children and the only part of her sister she had left.

When it came time for her small children, Renee and her husband had one each. The baby boy was reaching as he screamed, "Momma! I want Momma!"

The oldest one hollered, "Momma, wake up. Wake up, Mommy, wake up. Aunt Nay-nay, I want my momma to wake up. I want my momma."

No one was prepared as the youngest one began to reach in the coffin for Jarissa, screaming, "Mommy, come with me."

Renee pulled him back as her husband held onto the four-year-old. She had a hard time containing the youngster. He was screaming louder and harder than anyone for his momma. Renee's husband had to take the little one out the gym. Hearing her children call for her was by far the worse. They still didn't get the concept of their mother my best friend is gone, forever. O.B. tapped my arm when it was my time to view her.

The time had come. The irony is I arrest people for drugs and here lies my best friend, dead from drugs. Tears made their presence from my eyes. I didn't think I could do it. My friend helped me stand to my feet as he allowed his body to be my prop. It felt like my feet were made of bricks as they made a thumping sound. Going slow as ever, I came a few steps from her. Trembling and denial were now my best friends as O.B. continued to be beside me. Now I'm right here, close to the coffin and facing reality. Here, I saw her favorite saying on the inside of the coffin, "This is my Bye-Bye."

She had on our favorite color, blue, but hers was a deeper baby blue. It was her most admired long-sleeve lace, button-up shirt with the solid blue piece underneath. Today, her hair was in her usual candy curls, and she had a warm smile and her best friend locket about her neck. Her head was slightly tilted on her left hand as it was placed on her right shoulder,

261

while her right arm was lying softly on her stomach. My best friend looked like herself, just like Momma said she did. I wanted to reach up and touch her but couldn't. O.B. held me up as I cried out, "My best friend, my one and only true friend. I love you so much, J. I love you so much, J. Please don't leave me."

Showing out was unplanned but those feelings came out anyway. Suppressing those emotions were hard as I saw her lying before me so at peace with the choice she made. I faced O.B. and asked with tears, snot covering my face and not caring about onlookers, "How could she leave me? How could she leave us? How could she do this to me? I didn't say goodbye. The last thing she said to me was now she can sleep. I had no idea. I swear to God, I had no idea."

My state of mind was irrational and hurt as O.B. tried pulling me away. I reached for her. I didn't want to let my best friend go. I couldn't, because I know this is my last time seeing her. I couldn't move and I wasn't going to. My best friend lies ahead of me; she's gone and knowing she'll never speak to me again is a life changer. O.B. whispered, "Come on, Cat. Let her go."

I don't know what happened, but O.B. had me outside at a car. My mother came and she tried to help me, but I was crying too hard. Although, my eyes were aching from all the tears I had cried all week, being prepared for today was still a challenge. What all the people were saying to comfort me didn't work. My best friend is gone, and I can't believe it. Even after seeing her, I still can't face the fact that she is gone.

They pallbearers brought the body out as I was sitting in the car, unable to take it. Jackson caught another ride, and I didn't care anymore. O.B. was not going to let me be alone; he made me ride with him. I sat there like a lump, leaning on the door as he drove towards Union Grove Church on Old Jackson. I couldn't get out the car. I couldn't see them put her in the ground. That was too much for me and I know it.

Moments later, I heard the gun salute. With each shot, a tear fell. I had forgotten that she was in the National Guard for a year right after high school. Momma came and brought me the flag. When my mom got closer, she said, "Renee wanted you to have this."

I was surprised because she was Renee's only sibling. I took it and held it against my heart. Before Momma walked off, she put her hand on his shoulder and told O.B. to take me home and make sure I was safe. He shook his head yes as she went towards her truck. He said, "Come on, Cat. It's time to go."

"Okay," was softly spoken from my lips.

I didn't fuss about it; I just didn't care. On the way to my house, I saw my text from Texan. He told me that he was sorry, and he would keep me in prayer, because he knows how close she and I were. I only texted back thank you.

Bell asked, "You don't want to go to the repast?"

"No."

"Cat, you still need to be around your family."

"Between Beast, Jarissa and you, I have no real close friends."

"Cooley."

"He and I don't have history like I have with you all. I love him, but we are still in the early process of being together."

"It takes time."

"I don't want to deal right now. Momma knows I'm going home because she knows I always need to be alone when I grieve."

"You're not alone today."

I smiled because he always cheers me up. Thinking about his life, I asked, "You call her and tell her where you at?"

"I told her I was going to be with my family."

"Does she know it includes me too?"

"Yeah, she knows it includes mainly you."

"I'm not trying to break up a home."

"Cat, that was done the day I met you."

"You weren't with her then."

"I know. I only went after her because you didn't want me on that level and it still hurts some, but I'm a big boy."

"I'm glad you are here with me and thank you for being my friend, among anything else."

"Anything for you and that is why I'm here for you in your time of sorrow."

"What she say?"

"She didn't say anything. I would've come even if Cooley was here."

"How are you and your woman doing?"

"We shaky. Honestly, I should have waited, but I was hard-headed and didn't want to listen to you talk some sense into me. Jarissa even tried, but I told her she didn't know what she was talking about. Plus, I know she wants to leave me, because she knows how I feel about you."

"What have you told her that I haven't told him?"

"I told her even if you didn't love me; I couldn't love her as she needed, because the love just isn't there for her."

"Wow."

"Jarissa's death has done more than opened everyone's eyes, not only for you, but for me. I used to be quiet about how I feel, but not anymore."

"O.B. you can't love me."

"I can't, but I do. I'm cool with it. I understand our lives and as long as I get to have you as a friend, I'll be fine with that because you have been my dearest friend too."

"You're just trying to cheer me up."

"Yes, I am," he spoke with laughter. "But, on the real, you mean so much to me. You should be my wife."

"Should have but I'm not."

He drove towards my house in silence as I looked at the trees and admired the view.

CHAPTER 18

O.B. unlocked the door and I turned off the alarm. Soon as I walked in, I went straight to my room to change. Putting on a set of long pants pajamas, I went in the living room where O.B. was at. He was sitting in his favorite chair. I guess while I was changing, he changed into his jogging suit with the short sleeves. My friend and ex-lover, has been good to me. When I need a friend, we talk and if I need anything, he will do his best for me.

It's incredible that I don't love him like I should. O.B. knows he will always have a part of me and that is it. I'm in love with Cooley and I miss him dearly. If only things were different. No matter what I'd be going through, he was always there. I could tell him anything and he would listen unbiased, not like Cooley. The difference is I can't have them both. At that point, O.B. saw me and waved for me to come on in. I flopped down on the other end of the couch as he questioned, "You feeling better?"

"A little."

"At least you are doing a tad better."

"I need to know exactly what she knows."

He sat back and said, "She knows I love you and would be with you, if you'd have me."

"Really?"

"She knows our relationship is over, even if I don't have you. She knows I'm here with you and your family, because your cousin was like family to me."

"And what else?"

"She knows when I have been here with you, because she has followed me."

"Really!"

"Yeah, but all of this was when we were just friends."

"When did you tell her all this?"

"This morning before I left for the funeral, she came in the room and stared at me. I know she has loved me, but I only cared for her, and I have told her so. She was watching me get dressed as she asked me how I feel about you. I told her I love you and you mean the world to me. She moved out the door towards me and asked how you felt about me. I told her you don't love me like that and you would never come between us on purpose. She said I love my job and the people in it more than her and Cat, she is right. Admitting you don't love someone to their face is hard, especially when you should love them. She dropped her head and asked me in a weeping tone, why I strung her along in this relationship. I told her I didn't mean to. I truthfully thought I loved her and would never hurt her, because she is a great woman. I asked her to forgive me, and she didn't answer. She gave me a hug and told me goodbye."

"That was it?"

"Yeah. She knows I'm here."

"But it's not like that."

"I know and she knows. Every time she has asked me something, I told her the truth. What is the point in lying when you know what you are doing has consequences?"

"So, she is going to tell it, isn't she?"

"Probably."

"Ain't no probably to it. She is."

"You never told it?"

"No."

"Why?"

"I don't know what he and I have, to be honest with you. We go out, we go to church together, we only slept together once and now he is my boss."

O.B. was quiet. I added, "Look, nothing was official the last time I slept with you after my mom's party. I thought he was into Jarissa and that gave me the room to do what I wanted."

"I was a rebound?"

"No, I was lonely and in need. You happened to be there."

"What you going to tell him?"

"The truth."

"Which is?"

"I care about you and we are great friends."

"Cat, I love you and we were more than friends."

"We are friends now but if I don't have to tell him, I won't."

"You know that isn't going to happen. You gonna have to tell him."

"Before I tell him anything, allow me to enjoy myself and not think of situations, death or pain."

"What are you suggesting?"

Laughing, I asked, "You have any liquor?"

"Cat? Liquor?"

"I need to get messed up."

"That isn't going to accomplish anything."

"For right now, it's a hangover and a small time for me to forget about me. Never mind I have some vodka here."

Going in the kitchen, I got the liquor out the cabinet. I fixed two glasses of the mixed drink. Not even taking the cup at first, he waited before asking, "You sure you need to drink?"

"Right now, I don't know what I need."

He and I began to drink and laugh about the times we all had with Jarissa. He told me funny things that happened while I wasn't at work. It all sounded like stuff she would say or do. There was so much to hear as O.B. and I talked and drank all night long. On occasions, we would call in for pizza and we would eat. He was buying and I was having fun and without a care in the world.

The sun was coming up as he and I laughed and drunk more and more. I didn't know I had all this liquor until now. We woke up and drunk more and more. I have never drunk so much in my life. O.B. tried to out-drink me, but he couldn't. His skinny self couldn't hang. He passed out on me as I went out too. I don't know how long we were out, but the next thing I heard was a knock was at the door. It was the kind of knock that sounds like the police. Getting up, I mumbled, "I'm coming."

By glancing through the curtains, I could tell that it was night again. Looking over at O.B. it became obvious that we'd both passed out in the living room; he on one couch and me on the other. The knocking became even harder than before. Not even asking who it was, I opened the door, and it was Cooley. He stared at me in a strange way. I was unprepared when he pushed me to the side. I didn't know what to think as it hit me that Officer Bell was still here with me. Cooley took a glance around, then stated, "What, y'all have a private party?"

271

"No," I spoke, as his voice was loud, bothersome and accusatory.

Straightaway, he picked Bell up to his feet with one hand. Bell was in a disoriented state as we both heard, "You cheating on my sister with Catherine?"

"Huh?"

The pounding on Bell's head was making his body appear helpless. Cooley continued hammering punches as he yelled, "You slick bastard, answer me!"

Bell was in no condition to talk, because Cooley was getting the best of him. I'm still stunned. I didn't know Cooley could curse like that. Realizing what is going on, I ran over to them and stated, "Cooley, put him down and what are you talking about?"

His head didn't turn to me as he spoke viciously, "Catherine, shut the fuck up."

I assume from the way his head bobbed, Bell felt dizzy because his voice shook when he said, "C-Cooley, leave me alone, man."

Spitting back at O.B., Cooley roared, "You are not able to demand shit."

Cooley hit him a few more times like it was nothing. *His upper body strength is unbelievable*, I thought as he held

Bell up with one hand. From behind, I began pleading, "Put him down and let us talk about it."

"There is nothing to discuss if you aren't telling me the deal with you two."

"Cooley, it's not what you think."

Making a loud thud, Bell's body crumpled as Cooley threw him to the floor. Bell got up swinging. I tried breaking it up, but it was useless. The two men were hitting each other and tearing up my living room. Cooley was soon beating the life out of Bell, who stopped swinging. Cooley was having his way with Bell. I tried pulling Cooley off, but that didn't work. He didn't stop, so I ran to my room and got my personal nine. Going back into the living room, I ran to the door and fired a warning shot. Cooley released Bell's unresponsive body.

"Get up before I shoot you. I'm not thinking clearly, and I'm traumatized, so please get up!"

"So, you going to shoot me for your lover?"

"He isn't my lover, and I will not watch you kill him."

"So, he is that important to you?"

"It's not about importance, it's about right. Now, get up, Cooley," I said in my police tone.

Cooley eased off Bell, but not before giving him one final hit to the face. Bell continued to lay on the floor bleeding. I lowered my gun and Cooley's eyes met me with a cold hateful stare. He sounded disappointed when he asked, "You been seeing Bell the entire time, haven't you?"

I replied to those eyes peering into my soul, "No, it wasn't like that. I mean, I used to."

"Make up your mind. Either it is or it isn't."

"It used to be before he got married to your sister, then a few times after he got married. When I met you, I was only with him once and that was the night of my mother's party."

"You had sex the night I was going to come see you, but you were angry because I was counseling, Jarissa. I told her to hang close to me and not to get out of my sight. I told her that I would do my part to help her stay sober at the party, so she would not ruin it for you all by doing her drugs. She agreed. I tried to tell you, but you kept brushing me off. You didn't want to hear what I had to say, so I let you be mad until we could talk. I had no idea you thought that less of us; that less of me, but you did that."

I really felt stupid as I said, "I honestly thought you were feeling her, so I took it as my cue to do whatever."

"Is that the kind of action you would do if you were in a relationship?"

"I didn't know what we were. You never told me anything."

"Cat, I was trying not to rush you because of your commitment issues. You needed to feel comfortable with me and in our relationship. I didn't want you to rush into this with me and still be getting down on the side, but what good did that do? You still did it anyway."

"I was never with Bell like that."

"How about since me? Don't lie to me about how many times you were with that snake."

Shaking I stammered out the word, "Twice."

Cooley dropped his head and began kicking Bell. I tried haltering the attack, but he pushed me down. I knew Bell was unconscious. Rushing over to me in an angered state of mind, he got in my face as I was slumped on the floor. He was so close; I could feel his tears dripping onto my shirt. With watery eyes, he spat out, "You knew I loved you and you allowed him to help you hurt me and my sister."

"Cooley, I love you."

CHAPTER 19

He got up and pulled me behind him. He wouldn't look at me as he spoke. "You love me, but you walked in the funeral with your lover, in front of the entire Scott County PD, trying to make me look stupid. Who do you love because it's not me?"

"He wasn't my lover then, only my friend. That's all he has been to me lately. He knows of my feelings for you. Tonight, we didn't do anything but talk about Jarissa and drink. You have to take my word for it."

"Why should I, when you wouldn't believe my words about loving you?"

"Cooley, baby, please listen. You got to listen to me."

Crying like a baby, Cooley cleared his voice and spoke with anger. "No more listening, you've chosen your past over your future. When lover boy comes to, let him know my sister is filing for divorce. All his clothes will be outside on the ground when I leave. Wednesday, he will be transferred out my department on the grounds of hostile environment. You, on the other hand, will be gone to the Morton PD K-9 Unit on Friday. Enjoy yourselves."

He pushed me out the way by storming out without looking back. As he left my driveway, I fell against the door with chest pains. This couldn't be happening to me. When I'm innocent, he wants to trip but when I was doing something, he was quiet. I got off the door and went over to O.B., who lay beaten unconscious. I tried to see what degree his wounds were, and they didn't look life threatening. I got some water and damped his face with the towel. He moved and opened his eyes. The minute his eyes flew open, he smiled. Even in his condition, he said, "I guess we know she told it."

Returning his smile, I questioned, "Are you ok?"

"Help me off this floor."

Extending my hand, I helped him off the floor. He fell back onto the couch and sat there. Picking up the towel, I used the end of the towel to touch lightly around his eyes, nose and mouth. He touched my hand and said kindly, "Cat, I didn't think we would wake up like this."

"Be still and relax."

While he sat there with his eyes closed again and his head tilted, Bell tried going to sleep but out of fear of a concussion, I kept him awake. Two hours had passed, and I asked Bell, "How you feel?"

Lifting his head up a few inches, he added, "Like a mad man whipped me."

"One did."

Bell lifted his hand for me to help him up and I did. He wobbled a little, saying, "I have to go to the bathroom and shake this off me."

Like a good friend would, I helped him to the bathroom. He retorted, trying to do it on his own, "I got it from here, unless you want to hold it while I piss?"

"You right. You got it from here."

I closed the door and waited for him to finish. Almost thirty minutes later, he came out on his own with his face clear.

"He isn't going to jump on me for pussy I can't get."

"Don't do anything irrational."

"I'm not, but what'd he say about my wife?"

"He said she's getting a divorce; your clothes are on the ground, and he is transferring you on Wednesday and me on Friday."

"Where's he sending me?"

"He didn't say."

"Where are you going?"

"Morton PD, the K-9 Division."

"You knew you were going there but sending me off is some bull and you know it."

"I wouldn't advise you to talk to him just yet. He is angry."

"Hell, he didn't get whipped while he was out cold, drunk."

"Just take wherever he may send you. It could be a blessing in disguise."

"What about you?"

"What about me?"

"He should talk to you and not go by the past."

"I wish I'd told him so all of this could have been avoided."

We both were quiet and then Bell asked, "What do I do now?"

"You love your wife?"

"I care about her, but I love you."

"I don't love you like that."

"I know, Cat, it's Cooley; you love him."

"I do."

"You need to go see him."

"What about you?"

"Don't worry about me. I have some time, and I will use it to avoid going to work."

I got dressed and left Bell at my house. Heading across Highway 35, I went straight for Bell's house. Soon as I pulled up, I saw his wife. She gave me a glaring stare. Not paying attention to her facial expression, I asked, "Where is Cooley?"

"You need to get back in your truck and leave my yard, now."

"I don't want any trouble. I just want to see Cooley."

"It's bad enough you have my husband and now you want my brother too?"

"Please, tell me where Cooley is?"

"He will see you at the hospital if you don't leave!"

I got back in my truck and dialed his number over and over. He didn't answer and I didn't know what to think. I left their house and went back to mine. I got the mail and left the gate unlocked as I parked my truck. Bell was gone and I was all alone. Going inside, I only locked the door, not bothering to set the alarm and threw the mail on the table. Now, I wish I could call on Jarissa to talk to or chill out with.

Making up my mind, I showered and looked at the mail. My nerves covered me as they shook like leaves in the wind. There on the table was my letter from Jarissa. At first, I couldn't believe it and I didn't want to move but had to. Picking the letter up, my eyes teared up when I saw her handwriting. Sitting at my kitchen table, I took my time and opened the letter.

Not sure what to expect, I eased the folded paper out. My eyes watered. I don't know what to expect, because Renee got her letter and never told me what it said. In fact, I haven't talked to Renee that much to even ask her. Not knowing what to think, I opened it and started reading.

Hey girl,

I'm dead or about time you get this letter, I will be. I know you didn't think I would really kill myself, but I did. You thought you knew me, but you didn't. I got to the point of no return and decided to end it all, because my children would be better without me and so will the Scott County PD. As strange as it is, it is hard for me to put in terms all the things I need to say. I promised myself that I would not write a long, drawn-out letter and I will not.

You were my best friend, my ride or die and no matter how things went down between us, you kept how you felt real and for that, I envy you. You understood what I was going through, even if you didn't like it; you kept it real. Thank you and now for the purpose of this letter.

This letter is late because I asked the Postmaster to have it sent late for a reason. I had to make sure I was gone, so I wouldn't have to face you. For starters, I slept around with Bell one night, when he got drunk at my house. The entire time he thought it was you and might still think that 'til this day, but it was me. The next morning, he asked, and I didn't tell him any different. He was going on and on about how different but good sleeping with you were. It was awesome; just like you said he was.

I did it because he wanted you. I know; why I do it if I knew he wanted you? I did it because you always got the men that loved you for you; attitude and all. I could never understand why you. Then, there's Ve-Lo; your first love. I did him for the drugs, but it was neat to know he often thought my sex was better than yours and that is why I kept going back to him. His drugs weren't all that, but just knowing someone thought I was better than you sexually, made it worth the while.

Texan, he wouldn't do anything with me because he is fully committed to whatever you had going on with him. That didn't stop me from trying. He would say no all the time. Eventually, I gave up and stopped asking him. Even my baby daddy, when he was on you first. Although, he is locked up, he has told me that he wants you and only stayed with me because of the boys; don't I feel special? Still, you won.

Now, Cooley, he is a special case. I liked him, but he didn't feel me like that. Even though, I talked to him first he still ignored me. The only time he would talk to me is when he knew I was doing heroin, meth, crack and 'caine; yeah, I was doing it all and you didn't even know it. Whenever he knew I was strung out, he would take me under his wing and protect me. I thought if I was needy enough, he would feel sorry for me and give in, but he didn't. Regardless of the scheme I pulled, he seemed to see right through it.

As caring as he is, he was only feeling you, even though I told him of how you let men do their thing; he still had faith in you and your so-called relationship. I told him that if anything happened to me, you would be with Bell and if he wants to find you and Bell, he needs to go to your house, because you both will be drunk and passed out from a night of sex. Every time I was near Cooley, I would tell him all kinds of stuff about you. I was building him up to tear you down. He needed to see that you aren't the sweet girl he thinks you are.

He would only say that he'd wait until you tell him because he doesn't think you'd lie to him and how you have changed. I told him I would love to see the day; guess I won't. I'm the one that told Bell's wife about y'all, even when y'all weren't doing anything. I wanted someone to kick your ass for having it all, but no one did. You are more than likely angry with me right now, but I'm a dead woman, so how will I ever know and how can you ever tell me? You can't.

True, you have your great qualities, but you can be something serious and still they all wanted you. I was never good enough to attract real men. I didn't hate you, I hated being in the shadow of you. You are funny and level-headed, but I deserved to be happy. Honestly, the only thing I could beat you at is dying first and that is what I did. I decided to do this, so I wouldn't have to live in shame of the PD and be embarrassed by all the backstabbing I did to you.

I hope you find it in your heart to understand my reasons and believe that I believed my actions were justified. You once told me the earth would not be big enough for the both of us if I slept with him again. It wasn't and so I'm out.

Finally, your dad is a son of a bitch. He raped my mother and had Renee. Yup, she is your sister. How did I find this out? I overheard ya mom telling her husband. She probably forgot she'd told me to come over, because she wanted to talk to me about the indictment. Being family, I walked in the house and heard them in the back. When they finished, I made a noise so they could come out and they did, but it was too late, I had heard it all. I hope his ass kiss ass in hell.

> *Love you forever and ever,*
> *Jarissa*

I sat there unemotional as I read the letter repeatedly. Doing the next best thing, I called my mother and asked her. She couldn't deny it. My mother told me all about it and how she and my father only stayed married because of me and that hurt. She had to endure so much, because she wanted her family to stay together. It was only right to have Jarissa and

Renee to live with us after her sister died. She told me that Renee found out in her letter and wanted to wait until I got my letter before saying anything to me. I became a zombie. My best friend in the world had it in for me and I didn't know it.

My cousin is also my sister and to make it worse, Jarissa wanted to have what all I had. To me, I didn't have anything worth it. Calling Renee quickly entered my mind, but she never picked up. Although I dialed her back-to-back to back, she still didn't answer. Getting in my truck, I went to her house. When I pulled up, my mom's truck was there. They were on the back. I went inside and walked straight to the back to say, "Am I invited to this family reunion?"

They saw me and my mom stood up to hug me. She sat down and that was my signal to sit, which, I did. Renee didn't look at me because she was sobbing silently. My mom said, "Cat, I was just at the beginning of the story. As I was telling Renee, my husband did rape my sister."

My ears couldn't believe what I heard. My mom looked at me to say, "Your dad and I were mad at each other. I left him that day. I didn't know my sister was coming. When she did, she went to sleep in my bed. He was drunk and assumed she was me. He knew I had a sister, but he didn't know we were twins. She wasn't at our wedding because she was deployed. Anyway, he slept with her. The next morning, I came home and found them in bed. He was shocked. He told her she could press charges, because he was wrong. He apologized and it never happened again."

Momma stood up as she said, "It wasn't until she found out she was pregnant that she calculated it back; it was during the time she was with him. Her fiancé knew she got raped but she was still sleeping with him, so he assumed Renee was his. When Renee got sick as a child, that's when we found out about her paternity. By then, you were born and so was Jarissa. In fact, after Jarissa's father left; my sister had a wreck and was killed. That is how my nieces grew up with you. Your father wanted to tell you all, but I told him not to. I didn't want you all to look at him as a disgrace."

She didn't say anything else as I sat there in dismay. Renee, on the other hand, continued to stare out towards the trees in her back yard. I spoke, "I wouldn't have thought that, knowing the circumstances. What about you, Renee?"

"Right now, I'm at a loss for words. I read her letter to me and I couldn't believe it. I even asked Auntie, and she denied it at first, until I showed her the letter. She was just now telling me when you came over."

"How you feel about it?"

"There's nothing to feel. You still my family and I have always loved you like a sister."

"Jarissa only heard about him sleeping with her. She didn't hear about the entire story. Girls, I'm so sorry the information was kept from you all. I probably would've told it, but not now. You girls are all I have left, and I don't want to lose either one of you," Momma explained.

"Auntie, you won't. I hate Jarissa isn't here to hear all this."

I got up and Momma asked, "Where you going?"

"I need to go home and clear my mind. So much has happened and I need to process this on my own terms."

Renee got up and gave me a hug before I left. I didn't know how to take everything I'd just heard. I wanted to call Bell and talk to him, but I couldn't. Leaving out her driveway, I went home, still in need of having a conversation with someone. I called Cooley when I parked in my driveway. To my surprise, he picked up the phone by saying, "What do you want?"

"I really need to talk to someone."

"And why call me?"

"I know you will listen."

The line was quiet. He interrupted the quietness to say, "You called to talk, but you haven't said a word."

"I got my letter from Jarissa today and I know why you were upset."

"You were messing around with my sister's husband, then you slept with him while you and I were taking things slow."

"You right, but it wasn't like that at all. Bell has been a great friend to me and when you came over, that's all it was; two friends discussing another friend."

"That may have been true, but I don't know how many times he's laughed in my face and slept with the woman I fell for. Or how many times he's been talking to you and doing whatever, then sits at the table with my family, knowing the entire time he is in love with you too. Can you imagine how I felt or how it looked to my sister and me? You came to her house, knowing you've been sleeping with her husband."

"Whoa. When I came to her house, I wasn't sleeping with him then. What he and I had was before they got married and it wasn't like that on that level."

"I don't care what level it was on. What you want? I don't want to talk about us, because there is no us."

I became quiet as tears formed and my words threatened to choke me. "Just give me another chance to make it right. You won't be sorry if you do."

This time he was silent as he spoke coolly and calmly, "I don't think I can risk my heart to you again."

"Cooley, all I'm asking is that you do it. Trust me if you have never trusted me before. I know what I did was wrong, but I have learned from that mistake. That part of my life is over with. All you have to do is say you will have me back again."

He was quiet and didn't say anything as I waited for his answer. When he did speak, he said to me softly, "Cat, as much as I want to, I seriously can't trust you with something as important as my heart, which is attached to my love and my life. You came along and I loved again, when I didn't want to. I trusted again, when I thought there was no one else to make me smile. Not only did you come along and take my heart, you took that bitch and broke it. You made me rethink the way I did things. Since that has happened, I've searched myself to see if I could have done something different and my search came up the same. It wasn't me; it was you. The only fault I had was I loved someone that didn't want or need my love. So, now go do you. You don't need an excuse to do whatever or whoever anymore. I love you, but I'm going to get over you."

The line was quiet for a few seconds. Now I know how it feels to love someone, and they not love you as you should. For a long time, I have compared men to Ve-Lo, thinking they were all like him, but Cooley was different. Even when I saw he was different, I still pretended like he was like the other

289

men, I've played. I murmured, "Just forgive me and maybe in time you will let me back into your life."

"I can forgive you, but I'm not so sure about letting you back in my life. Just go and find what you looking for in life and maybe, just maybe—"

"Just maybe what?"

"I don't know. I'm just saying, just maybe, things between us can change, then again, maybe it won't. Or maybe, just maybe; we go our separate ways forever. Goodbye, Cat."

He didn't give me a chance to tell him goodbye. He hung up as if he didn't want to hear me say it. Silently, I sat back in the seat and cried. I haven't cried this hard over a man, not since Ve-Lo and here I am, crying harder than ever. I believe it's because I'd fallen in love, and I chose to play him like the rest. Now, I'm ending up like the rest. Alone.

Epilogue

Cat entire objective on life changed. She gave Beast to the Morton K 9 Unit and became an investigator. While Cooley continued as the Captain of the Sheriff Department, crime became less in the county. Cat joined the church to better herself and, in the process, she and Cooley reunited. They made Jesus their foundation and got married. A year later Cooley and Cat had a little girl named Whitley Jayce.

Renee had a girl named her Kaitlin Jareese. She later left the police department to become a Behavior counselor to young adults.

Having custody of Jarissa's children brought her and Cat closers friends and sisters.

Bell tried rekindling his marriage, but it didn't work. They divorced and he transferred to Hancock County Police Department; where he stayed focused and remarried.